The Murder of Sleepy Hollow

A Charlie Kingsley Mystery

Books by Michele Pariza Wacek
MPWnovels.com/books

Secrets of Redemption series:
It Began With a Lie (Book 1)
This Happened to Jessica (Book 2)
The Evil That Was Done (Book 3)
The Summoning (Book 4)
The Reckoning (Book 5)
The Girl Who Wasn't There (Book 6)
The Room at the Top of the Stairs (Book 7)
The Secret Diary of Helen Blackstone (free novella)

Charlie Kingsley Mystery series:
A Grave Error (free prequel novella)
The Murder Before Christmas (Book 1)
Ice Cold Murder (Book 2)
Murder Next Door (Book 3)
Murder Among Friends (Book 4)
The Murder of Sleepy Hollow (Book 5)
Red Hot Murder (Book 6)
A Wedding to Murder For (novella)
Loch Ness Murder (novella)

Stand-a-lone books:
Today I'll See Her (novella)
The Taking
The Third Nanny
Mirror Image
The Stolen Twin

The Murder of Sleepy Hollow

A Charlie Kingsley Mystery

by Michele Pariza Wacek

ISBN 978-1-945363-49-8

Library of Congress Control Number: 2022948090

For my family, for always believing in me.

Chapter 1

This is NOT a date, I told myself again as I approached the doors of The Tipsy Cow, Redemption's best, most happening bar.

Yes, it was true I was meeting Officer Brandon Wyle in said bar. But we were meeting for lunch, not a drink. The Tipsy Cow had surprisingly good food.

Besides, he had already made the point clear. It was about a case he wanted some help with, although that alone was enough to raise my suspicions. Up until this point, Wyle had never appreciated my help with his investigations. He would prefer I focus on my little home-based tea and tincture business and leave the investigating to the "professionals."

Quite honestly, I wouldn't mind that, either. I'd love to concentrate solely on growing the herbs and flowers I used in my teas and on baking and cooking in my big farmhouse kitchen. But, as it turned out, I had a bit of a knack for solving cases. And that talent ended up coming in handy for my tea customers, as some of them had a knack for finding trouble.

Usually, Wyle begrudgingly accepted my help, mostly because he knew once I got involved, there wasn't much he could say to talk me out of it. But we also had a clear understanding that I'd keep him in the loop.

So, for him to bring me in on a case was … strange. I wasn't sure what to make of it. I was also too curious to not agree to meet him.

Even though I was clear on the purpose of the meeting, I still found myself taking a little extra time with my appearance that morning. Well, okay, a lot of extra time. I ended up going through most of my closet before settling on jeans and an emerald-green sweater that brought out the green in my hazel eyes. I paired it with a clunky gold necklace and big gold hoops and left my wild and curly brownish-blondish hair loose around my shoulders. I even applied a little makeup—some mascara and lip gloss.

Not too much. Because, of course, this was *not* a date.

But that didn't mean I couldn't look nice.

I also wore my jean jacket, as it was fall in Wisconsin, so it was nippy. Early October was so beautiful, with the leaves changing colors and the temperature cool, but not bitterly cold. That would come later.

Parking around The Tipsy Cow was full, which didn't surprise me, as it always had a brisk lunch crowd. I had to park a little ways down the street, and as I walked to the bar and grill, I checked the cars to see if Wyle's was there yet. I didn't see it, which didn't necessarily mean he hadn't arrived. He could've parked somewhere else other than on the street. However, when I opened the front door and surveyed the bar, I wasn't completely surprised not to see him.

"Would you like a table?" the young, perky hostess asked as I stood in the foyer frowning and scanning the area. She looked like a cheerleader with her dark-blonde hair pulled up in a high, bouncy ponytail and bright smile. Only the line of piercings that outlined her ears betrayed the image.

I chewed on my lip. Did I want a table? On one hand, we were there to eat, so getting one seemed to make sense. On the other, it felt a little too … something. I would have to admit to Miss Perky that I was waiting for someone, and she might then assume it was a date, which it wasn't. And what if he didn't show up? It was possible he got pulled away and couldn't leave the station. And then I would be sitting by myself at a table, and the hostess would know I had been stood up.

"I'm waiting for someone, but I can just sit at the bar," I told her. The bar had a full view of the door, so not only would I see him, but he would see me when he walked in. That felt a little less assuming.

"Of course," the hostess said with a big smile. I gave her an awkward nod in return and headed to the bar.

It was too early for a drink, so I ordered a Coke with lemon. I perched on the edge of the stool, shrugged off my jacket, and looked around.

As it was early, there weren't many people in the bar. Most were sitting at tables eating lunch. An older guy drinking a beer and eating a hamburger was at the opposite end of me. He seemed to be a regular, as he was chatting with the bartender. Another man sat alone at a table, a beer and bunch of papers and folders strewn about in front of him. He muttered to himself as he pawed through them, occasionally taking a sip from his bottle. Every time he set it back down, it was closer to his papers. I kept watching, fascinated despite myself, wondering if he was going to end up knocking it over. He was tall and gangly, all legs and arms and elbows, and didn't seem to be paying attention to his surroundings at all.

I had about decided I really ought to say something to him when it happened—his arm flew forward to grab a different folder, except he whacked his beer at the same time. It toppled to its side, spilling the contents across his papers. He leaped to his feet, tipping his chair over while knocking some of them onto the ground.

He swore as he desperately tried to save the pages from the puddle of beer. I grabbed a stack of napkins from the bar and slid off my chair to help him.

"How stupid," he was saying as he shook the papers. "I can't believe I did this. What an idiot."

As I mopped up the beer, I tried to reassure him. "Hopefully, we can save most of it," I said.

"Yeah, well ..." He looked sadly at the soaking wet papers in his hand. "It serves me right. I'm such a klutz. I should have known this was going to happen." He glanced up and flashed me a shy smile. I caught my breath. He was surprisingly good-looking in a geeky sort of way, with his messy light-brown hair falling across his forehead, straggly goatee, and horn-rimmed glasses.

"Maybe you should have gotten a bigger table," I suggested as I continued piling the used napkins on the table.

He laughed. "More room for me to make a bigger mess."

The bartender appeared behind me, bar rag in hand, and suggested moving to a different table, so he could clean up. It took a bit to help the man move, as we laid the worst of the drenched pages flat on the table to help them dry. Eventually, though, he settled on one nearby. The bartender even brought him a second beer.

"I think I'm going to drink first, then work," he said, shaking his head at the wet pages. "Or maybe I should say, 'hopefully' work. Once things dry."

"It looks like most of the pages are somewhat legible," I said. "So, maybe you can transfer the data somewhere else."

"Yeah, that's what I'll have to do." He sighed and glanced up at me with another shy smile. "Can I buy you a drink? It's the least I can do, to thank you for your help."

"I already have a soda," I answered.

He gestured to the seat next to him. "Do you want to have a seat?"

I bit my lip and glanced around the bar. Still no sign of Wyle. "I'm meeting someone," I hedged.

"I won't stop you from leaving when he arrives," he said. "Or is this a nice way of telling me to buzz off, and I'm just not getting the hint?"

That made me laugh. "Okay, I guess it can't hurt to keep you company while I wait." I started to turn back toward the stool to fetch my jacket, purse, and drink, but paused. "How did you know I was meeting a 'he'?"

His smile widened, crinkling the skin at the corners of his eyes. "Well, I had a fifty-fifty shot of being right. So, I guess this means you do have a date."

"Not a date," I said hastily. "Just friends … sort of. It's complicated."

His eyebrows went up. "Oh, one of those relationships."

"No, not one of those," I said, flustered. I could feel my cheeks starting to burn. "He's just … it's more professional than anything else. Never mind. I'll just grab my stuff." Feeling like an idiot, I went to get my things and then sat down in the seat next to him, so I could still keep an eye on the door.

"I'm Ike, by the way," he said. "Ike Krane."

"Charlie Kingsley," I said.

"Nice to meet you, Charlie," he replied. "I take it you live here."

"Is it that obvious?"

He smiled, and his eyes crinkled again. "Well, I confess, your meeting someone here for some sort of 'professional' lunch was a big clue," he said. "So, what is it you do?"

"I make teas and tinctures," I said.

He looked surprised. "Oh. That's interesting. So, you do consults, then? About the types of tea someone might want?"

"Sometimes," I said. "I do make custom blends, depending on what a person is looking for. But I also have pre-blended teas that are very popular. Like my lemon and lavender and Deep Sleep teas. Nearly all my customers want those. Why, are you looking for something custom?"

"Honestly, I've never thought about having one made," he said. "But maybe I should. I take it your lunch companion is looking for something custom, too."

"Oh, Wyle? No, he's not a huge tea drinker," I smiled at the thought. While it was true Wyle would drink my tea when he came over to discuss cases, he was mostly interested in the cookies and other baked goods I always had on hand.

Ike's expression was puzzled. "Oh. I just assumed, since you said it was a professional meeting."

"Oh, that." I was feeling flustered again. "No, I'm helping him with a case."

His eyes widened. "A case? Like a private investigator type of case?"

"Sort of." I was really uncomfortable now, especially since I could picture Wyle cringing at the words. He had mostly resigned himself to me helping on an unofficial basis, but he would hate people thinking it was anything sanctioned. Not because he cared about who got credit, but because he didn't want me to either inadvertently mess up the case or become a target. "He's a cop. I sometimes help him with his cases."

"Oh, so *you're* the private investigator."

I shook my head. "It's nothing like that. Strictly amateur, I assure you."

"Ah." He cocked his head as he studied me. "You must be pretty good, then."

"It's a gift," I admitted, smiling.

"Maybe I need to work with you," Ike said.

"Why, are you in some sort of legal trouble?"

A cloud seemed to pass over his face, but almost as quickly, it disappeared, leaving me to wonder if I had imagined it. "Actually, I was thinking more about combining forces. I'm an investigator, too."

"Really? You're a private investigator?"

"In a way, I suppose. I investigate ghosts."

"Ghosts?" It was my turn to give him a confused look. "People hire you to investigate hauntings?"

He smiled. "Sometimes. I used to do a lot more of that a few years back. Now, I focus mostly on investigating famous ghost hauntings around the country."

"Well, that explains why you're in Redemption, then." All the way back to its founding in 1888, Redemption had a long history of being a strange and haunted town. All the adults disappeared that winter, leaving only the children. Since then, the town had been plagued by more than its share of mysterious disappearances, odd occurrences and, of course, murders.

"Yeah, Redemption has definitely been at the top of my list for some time. I'm excited to finally make it here."

"You'll definitely stay busy," I assured him.

He did that eye-crinkling thing again. "Good. I like being busy."

I glanced toward the door, wondering where Wyle was. Even though I was enjoying my conversation with Ike, I was also starting to feel a little uneasy. Especially with the way he was looking at me. It had been a while since a man openly flirted with me. Whatever the apparent connection between Wyle and I was didn't count. Honestly, I wasn't at all sure what to do with it, anyhow. "So, once you investigate these famous places, then what?"

He let out a laugh. "Oh, I guess I forgot that part. I'm a writer."

"Really?" Now I was definitely uneasy, but for a very different reason. "For a publication?"

"If you define books as publications, then yes," he said as he sipped his beer. "I have a series where I write about haunted places in America. I go investigate different places and document my findings."

"So, you're going to write about Redemption?"

"That's the plan. My next book is about famous hauntings in the Midwest so, of course, Redemption is near the top of the list."

I nodded, still feeling bothered. I had a bad feeling about where this was going. "Focusing on any places in particular?"

His face lit up as he started pawing through the papers on the table. "Yes. There are a few local legends I want to track down ... one is called 'Fire Cabin.'" He glanced up at me. "Have you heard of it?"

"I have," I said. I decided I didn't need to mention my last case, where five friends went into the woods looking for Fire Cabin, but only four returned.

"That one, for sure," he said, turning his attention back to his notes. "There's also a local bar that burned down. Lone Man Standing, I think it was called?"

"Yes, I'm familiar with that bar," I said, also deciding not to mention that I had a memorable run-in with Red, the owner, before he disappeared. Everyone assumed he died in the fire. I wasn't so sure.

"I know it's gone now, but I was thinking the area around it might still be haunted," he said. "While fire is good at destroying things, depending on what exactly is haunted, or if there's anything left, there still might be something there."

"It's definitely worth checking out," I said, the knot in my stomach becoming tighter. I was dreading what else he would mention.

"Oh, and the haunted houses, of course," he added. "There are quite a few of them, which of course makes sense in such a haunted town. The one at the top of my list is Helen Blackstone's. I definitely MUST check out her house."

And there it was. *My* house. And the absolute last thing I wanted was for it to be written up in any book.

I cleared my throat. "Actually, Helen Blackstone doesn't own that house anymore."

His eyebrows went up. "Oh?"

"Yes, she sold it."

His brow furrowed. "That isn't in my notes." He started shuffling through his papers. "How do you know?"

"Because I'm the one who bought it," I confessed.

Now I had his full attention. He sat up straight and stared at me. "You? You own Helen Blackstone's house?"

"I do."

He beamed at me. "Oh, this is my lucky day! I guess it was a good thing I spilled my beer."

I smiled back, but it was forced. "Good thing," I repeated, although inside, I was wondering if it was less about luck and more about Redemption deciding to put us together. Along with all the other strange happenings, many of the local townspeople were convinced that Redemption itself decided who stayed and who didn't. I personally didn't believe it, but on the other hand, I couldn't account for all the odd coincidences that had to align for me to end up a permanent resident.

Ike was so excited, he didn't notice my less-than-enthused response. "I can't believe the sale wasn't in my records. When did that happen?"

"About three years ago," I said.

He fumbled through his belongings until he located a pen. He pulled the cap off with his teeth and started to jot down a few notes. "Were you already living here then?"

"No, I was passing through."

He wasn't looking at me, still busily writing things down. "Where are you from?"

"New York."

He stopped writing and looked at me. "Really? That's where I'm from. Where in New York?"

"Manhattan," I said.

"Oh, the city," he said. "I'm from a little town outside of there."

"Where?" I asked. "We did a lot of traveling around New York when I was a kid, so I might recognize it."

Now it was Ike's turn to make a face. "It's pretty small. You wouldn't know it."

He definitely had my attention. "Try me."

He shifted uncomfortably in his seat. "Sleepy Hollow."

My eyes went wide. "Really? Talk about a haunted city. Is living there what got you interested in ghost hunting?"

"You could say that," he said drily. "That and my parent's sense of humor."

I tilted my head. "What do you mean?"

He sighed. "My last name is Krane, although it's spelled K-r-a-n-e."

I looked at him in confusion for a moment, before it all made sense. "Ike? Is that short for Ichabod?"

He sighed again.

"Oh, wow." I stared at him in amazement. "I know it's a fictitious story, but is there an actual Ichabod Crane? And are you related to him?"

"As far as I know, it's all a product of Isaac Washington's imagination," Ike said. "But regardless, our last names ARE spelled differently."

"Right. Of course."

He looked at me, one side of his mouth curled up. "You shouldn't laugh. You have no idea what it's like growing up as Ike Krane in Sleepy Hollow, New York."

"I'm sure it was challenging," I said, trying not to smirk.

"Yes, it was," he affirmed. "And trust me, my folks were not much help."

"That does seem a little brutal, to name your son after a fictional character who disappeared after a run-in with the Headless Horseman," I said. "Weren't they afraid to tempt fate?"

"Along with having a warped sense of humor, they are also firm nonbelievers in ghosts, hauntings, and anything else paranormal," he said. "I think naming me Ike was another way to spit in the eye of Sleepy Hollow's ghostly reputation." He waggled his eyebrows.

I laughed. "They must be so proud of your career."

He snorted. "Yes, my becoming a ghost hunter was MY way to spit in their skeptical eye." His expression turned more serious. "Quite honestly, I'm not a huge believer in ghosts, either."

I shot him a curious look. "A ghost hunter who doesn't believe?"

He shrugged. "I know. It sounds weird. But I do think it's helped me more than not. I come into each situation expecting to debunk the ghosts and hauntings."

"And do you?"

He sipped his beer. "For the most part, yes."

"The most part? So there are times you haven't?"

"I would say there have been times when the results haven't been conclusive."

"But that's not enough to convince you that ghosts exist?"

"I said the results were inconclusive, which means they weren't conclusive either way. That ghosts exist or don't exist."

"Of course," I said, nodding.

He sat back and studied me. "Although I don't know why I'm trying to convince you. You not only live in Redemption, but in a notoriously haunted house. I mean, yours isn't just any haunted house ... it's the most haunted in Redemption. You're probably a big believer, I'm guessing."

"Well ..." I started.

His expression was shocked. "You don't believe?"

"I think the truth is more complicated," I said. "While it's true I've had some strange ... encounters in that house, I also think that the way ghosts reveal themselves is a little different from what most ghost stories lead us to believe."

My house was built back in the early 1900s by a rich man to impress his new bride, Martha. It didn't go very well, as she ended up killing her maid and then herself. It's her ghost who still allegedly haunts my house to this day. Then again, it could also be Nellie, the maid who was purportedly having an affair with Martha's husband. I supposed who the ghost is, or even if it were both of them, didn't really matter. The bottom line is that the townspeople continued to consider it one of the most haunted places in Redemption.

My personal dealings with the ghosts were pretty minimal—a few unexplainable occurrences and some peculiar dreams. For the most part, the ghost (or ghosts) left me alone, and I left them alone. It seemed to work out just fine for all of us.

Ike, however, seemed puzzled by my response. "What do you mean? How did the ghosts show themselves to you?"

I paused, contemplating how to explain it. "More subtly, I guess," I said. "It's less in your face, so to speak, like what you see in the movies. It's more about a ... a feeling. Or a different way of communicating, through dreams or the way certain events line up. I personally haven't seen anything, although I suppose it's possible that some people are more ... sensitive, maybe? And again, I think a lot of times, if there *is* something haunting a place, it reveals itself in more subtle ways than jumping out from behind a corner and yelling 'boo.'"

"Well, I will say, in my professional opinion, ghosts rarely say 'boo.'" Ike said gravely. "Still, you make a good point. That could also mean there are more haunted places than we even know of, simply because we don't know what to look for."

"That's possible," I agreed. "I hadn't thought about it like that." From the corner of my eye, I saw the door to the bar swing open and Wyle step through. "Oh. I have to go," I said, gathering my things.

Ike glanced over to the front of the bar. "So that's your lunch date," he said.

"It's not a date," I insisted as I got to my feet.

"Of course not," Ike replied as I looked over toward Wyle. He was staring at us, a scowl on his face. I could feel my heart sink.

"I have to go," I repeated. "I hope you'll be able to get your investigating done."

"Oh, I will," Ike said, flashing a smile at me. "And don't worry … I'll be in touch. The most haunted house of Redemption is definitely getting special treatment from me."

Great. That was all I needed.

I didn't even respond as I made my way over to a very unhappy-looking Wyle. This was going to be an awesome lunch.

Chapter 2

"Who is that?" Wyle demanded as soon as I reached him.

"Let's get a table, and I'll fill you in," I said with a sigh. I turned, and the blonde, too-young hostess was watching our exchange with a little too much interest for my taste.

"Table for two?" she chirped.

"Could we get a booth in the back?" Wyle asked, flashing one of his devastating smiles at Miss Perky.

She flushed, her cheeks turning a very attractive shade of pink. "Of course, officer. Something a little more private. Right this way."

Wonderful. Now the hostess thought we were dating, and worse, that I had been caught doing something wrong by chatting with Ike while I waited.

I gritted my teeth as I followed her to our table. This day was getting better and better. If I could have canceled right then and there and run out of the bar, I would have done it in a heartbeat. But I was going to have to face Wyle sooner or later, so it might as well be sooner.

"So, who was that?" Wyle asked once the hostess had departed. He flipped open the menu but didn't look at it.

"Nice seeing you, as well, Wyle. No, of course it's not a problem you were running late. I didn't mind waiting at all," I said, my words dripping sarcasm.

Wyle's expression shifted into something more like embarrassment. "I didn't mean to make you wait," he said. "I'm a cop. Things come up. I can't always show up at a scheduled time."

"I get it," I said. "And I'm not trying to rag on you for running late. Just like you shouldn't rag on me for talking to someone while I waited for you."

He gave me a long look. "Are you trying to tell me you started flirting with a stranger because you were bored?"

13

"I was hardly flirting," I said. "I was having a conversation with a tourist."

He didn't look convinced. "It looked like a little more than a simple conversation from where I was standing. Are you sure he didn't ask you out?"

"Positive," I answered, although remembering the interest in Ike's eyes, I could feel my cheeks start to warm.

Wyle noticed it, as well. "He *did* ask you out, didn't he?"

I held my hands out. "Look. We've had this conversation before. I'm not interested in dating anyone, let alone someone who is in Redemption to investigate ghosts. I made it clear I was only talking to him while I waited for you, and I wasn't interested in anything else."

Wyle's eyes sharpened. "He investigates ghosts?"

I looked at him in exasperation. "That's all you heard?"

"I heard all of it," Wyle said. "We can get back to the flirtation later, but I have questions about the ghost investigating."

The waitress appeared at that moment, leaving me sputtering in my seat. Her brown hair was pulled back in a messy ponytail, and her face was puffy and tired, making her look older than she probably was. Wyle flashed her a dazzling smile and told her we needed a minute to choose from the menu, but only a minute, as he had to get back to work. I ended up ordering the Cobb salad, as it was known to be surprisingly good. Wyle chose the Reuben.

"So, tell me more about this ghost investigator," he said.

"First, tell me why you're suddenly so interested," I countered.

"It will make more sense if you tell me first," Wyle said.

I shot him a look.

Wyle sighed. "Fine. It has to do with why I asked you to lunch. There's been some … strange occurrences going on."

I perked up. "Strange occurrences?" Maybe Wyle really was going to bring me on to a case.

He nodded. "Although keep in mind it's October, and Halloween is right around the corner. Strange occurrences do happen more often in Redemption around this time of year. Still, it just seems to be … more than usual. And a little earlier, as well."

"Like what happens at the graveyard?" One of the many strange Redemption tales had to do with the graveyard, where apparently, the week before Halloween, the gargoyle statues have been known to come to life and wander around. Teenagers laid bets as to who could stay in the graveyard after dark the longest, and, most of the time, they didn't last long.

I had my own run-in with the gargoyles at the cemetery last year, and quite frankly, I wasn't interested in a repeat performance.

"Sort of," Wyle said. "In that same vein, anyhow. Now, tell me more about this ghost investigator."

"I think he called himself a ghost 'hunter,'" I clarified.

Wyle rolled his eyes. "Whatever. Who is he?"

"His name is Ike Krane," I said. "He's from Sleepy Hollow, New York."

Wyle stared at me. "Ike Krane. Like Ichabod? And he's from Sleepy Hollow?"

"Exactly. Although he spells Krane with a K instead of a C. Apparently, his parents had a dreadful sense of humor. Anyway, Ike decided to embrace his namesake and become a ghost hunter. He goes around the country investigating haunted places and then writing and publishing his experiences in a book. He's doing one on Midwestern hauntings, so of course, he's here in Redemption."

Wyle was still staring at me, a fairly shocked expression on his face. I was about to ask him what was bothering him when our drinks arrived.

He was the first to speak after the waitress left. "Do you know when he got here?"

"I didn't ask," I said. "Why?"

Wyle craned his neck to look past me. "I should see if he's still around," he said, starting to slide out of the booth.

"Wyle? What is going on?" I asked, but he was already striding away toward the bar.

I turned back around in frustration. What was with him? First, he seemed almost jealous of Ike, and now, he was basically acting like the man was some sort of criminal.

What was going on?

I didn't have long to stew over it because Wyle was back in a few minutes. "He's already gone," he fretted as he slid back into his booth. "I don't suppose you know where he's staying?"

I glared at him. "Why would I know that? I started this conversation by telling you I had no interest in going on a date with him, so of course I wouldn't ask where he's staying."

One side of Wyle's mouth curved into a smile. "Probably the Redemption Inn. I'll call over there, now that I know his name."

I was so frustrated, I wanted to reach across the table and throttle him. "What is going on? Why are you going through all this effort to track down some ghost hunter?"

Wyle picked up his Coke to take a drink, eyeing me from over the glass rim. I got the impression he was enjoying keeping me in suspense.

If he kept it up much longer, he might find himself wearing that Coke.

"We've been getting some odd reports," Wyle finally said, but before he could go any further, the waitress appeared with our food. I gritted my teeth.

"What odd reports?" I asked as soon as she left.

Wyle picked up his Reuben. "Someone has been leaving jack-o-lanterns in people's yards."

"Jack-o'-lanterns?" I looked at him in bewilderment. "You mean like carved pumpkins?"

He nodded. "Exactly like that."

"Well, that's … weird," I said. It *was* weird, but not overly malicious. Why would Wyle invite me to lunch to talk about this? "Is that all?"

He shook his head as he swallowed a bite of food. "A couple of them have also found, well, pumpkin guts, I guess, for lack of a better term, strewn all over their porches."

"Ugh, that would be unpleasant to clean up." It would probably start to smell, too, after a while. Like rotten pumpkin. Not pleasant.

"You're telling me," Wyle said. "I went out to look at a couple of the houses. It was a real mess."

"I bet." I moved some lettuce around my plate. "I get that it would suck if it happened to you, but honestly, this sounds more like a bunch of kids playing a prank."

Wyle nodded as he swallowed another bite. "That's what we thought, as well. Like toilet papering a yard, except with pumpkins, in honor of Halloween."

I stabbed a piece of chicken. "Makes sense to me. But I'm still not seeing how Ike fits into this, or why you would ask me to lunch to tell me about it. Do you think I know the teenagers who are responsible, or something?"

"I'm getting to that. Sorry," he said through a mouthful of food. "I hate to eat and run, but I have to get back to the station."

"No problem," I assured him, but inside, I was feeling a little let down. Which made no sense. This wasn't a date, after all. It was a work lunch.

"Anyway," Wyle continued after he swallowed. "One of the things I noticed was that all the houses that have been targeted have a reputation of being haunted. Of course, I immediately thought that was more evidence of the whole thing being some kind of prank. You know how kids get around Halloween and haunted houses."

"I do," I said, although for the most part, they left my house alone. I think they were all a little too afraid of it … or of me. There were rumors I was a witch who made potions in my kitchen. All nonsense, of course, but that didn't stop the rumors from persisting.

"I wanted to warn you this was going on, so you could keep an eye out."

"I appreciate that," I said.

"But then ..." Wyle took another bite. "We started to get reports about horses galloping down the streets."

"Horses ... galloping?"

Wyle nodded. "In the middle of the night. People would be woken by the sound of horse hooves hitting the pavement and loud neighing."

I started to get a bad feeling about where this was going. "Someone is riding a horse around in the middle of the night?"

"That's what it sounds like. Except ..." Wyle paused dramatically to take a drink of his Coke. "When they look out the window, there's no horse to be found."

I stared at Wyle. "You mean ... like a ghost horse?"

"Yes, like a ghost horse," Wyle said. "That was exactly what the homeowners were thinking. Of course, it made no sense. There have never been reports of a ghost horse in Redemption before. At least, none that anyone remembers. So, why now? Where would a ghost horse come from?"

The pieces were clicking into place. "You think someone ... brought a ghost horse to Redemption?"

Wyle flashed me a sideways smile. "Don't you think this all bears more than a passing resemblance to the Headless Horseman?"

Chapter 3

Jack-o'-lanterns. The sound of a horse galloping at night. A ghost hunter from Sleepy Hollow named Ike Krane.

It seemed way too pat.

"You honestly think a fictional story has come to life? In Redemption?"

Wyle shrugged. "I think someone might be trying to make it *appear* like a fictional story has come to life in Redemption."

"And you think that person is Ike?"

"It makes sense," Wyle said. "You said he was an author, right? What better way to generate buzz about his books than to claim he's being followed by the Headless

Horseman?"

"Yes, but that's TOO obvious," I said. "People would assume he's making it up."

"Maybe," Wyle agreed. "I didn't say it would necessarily work. It's possible he's giving it a trial run here in Redemption. Redemption has so many strange things that happen as it is— what's one more rumor going to hurt?"

"I don't know," I said, my voice skeptical. "I don't buy it."

He gave me a hard look. "Why? Because it doesn't seem like something Ike would do? Because you know him so well?"

"Don't be such a jerk," I said. "Because I don't see how he could possibly get away with it. Everyone would assume he's behind it, so why do something so stupidly obvious?"

"Maybe that's the point," Wyle said.

I rolled my eyes. "That makes even less sense."

"Think of it like a marketing stunt," Wyle said. "It's a joke. He knows it's a joke; we know it's a joke. It's all fun and games. It still gets people's attention, right? And he can then pivot right to talking about his new book."

"Maybe," I said, although remembering how Ike had talked about growing up with his name, it didn't seem like he wanted people to connect the dots between him and the famous story. Of course, continuing Wyle's theory, that could be part of the act, as well.

"Regardless, I think asking him a few questions is in order," Wyle said, wiping his mouth with a napkin and reaching for the check.

"How much do I owe?" I asked as Wyle dug through his wallet, but he waved me off.

"It's the least I can do, as I was late," he said, pulling out some cash.

"You don't have to do that," I offered, feeling uncomfortable at the thought of him buying me lunch.

"I know I don't have to," he answered, placing a few bills on the table and shooting me a crooked smile that made my heart stutter. "But I want to."

I wasn't sure what to say, so I concentrated on stabbing my salad.

"Besides," he continued. "I think I owe you about a million meals for all the times you've cooked for me."

It felt like he had doused me with ice water. Was that what this was? Him paying back a debt?

He tucked his wallet in his back pocket, seemingly oblivious to how cold I had instantly become. "I'll keep you posted on what I find out," he said, sliding out of the booth. "In the meantime, you might want to keep an eye out for stray jack-o'-lanterns, in case it IS kids after all."

"I'll do that," I said into my salad as he sauntered away.

Argh. I turned my attention back to my plate, although my appetite had disappeared. What a frustrating day.

***

"Of course," Pat mused as she reached for one of my home-made chocolate chip cookies. Tiki, her white toy poodle, followed her hand with her nose. "The jack-o'-lanterns. The horse galloping. Of course it's the Headless Horseman. I can't believe I missed it."

I stared at her. "Wait. You knew about this?"

Pat stared back. "You didn't?"

We were sitting in my large farmhouse kitchen at the butcher-block table, cups of tea and chocolate chip cookies in front of us. The afternoon sun shone through the large window that overlooked the garden. Midnight, my black cat, napped on one of the chairs that was strategically placed under that window.

After the lunch fiasco, I decided I needed some tea, something sweet, and a sympathetic ear. Inviting Pat over was a no-brainer. Except, I didn't seem to be getting the sympathy I had hoped for. I was starting to wonder if this was just going to be one of those days, and my best move would be to send Pat home, lock the doors, and crawl into bed. Hopefully, the next day would be less frustrating.

Pat was a good decade or so older than me, and the best way to describe her was "round." She was plump, with a round face, round, black-rimmed glasses, and short, no-nonsense brown hair that was turning gray. She had been one of my first tea customers and had since become one of my best friends, as well as my partner in crime-solving.

"No, I hadn't heard a thing about jack-o'-lanterns or horses galloping at night," I said. "When did you get wind of it?"

"Just the other day," Pat said, breaking off a piece of cookie to feed to Tiki. Today, Tiki was wearing a bright-orange sweater with matching orange ribbons in her fur. Pat had announced that since it was starting to get chilly outside, Tiki needed a sweater. It was no longer optional, but necessary that she dress her little dog up.

Luckily, Tiki didn't seem to mind.

"Don't give Tiki the chocolate chip cookies," I said, pushing over a second plate. "Here. Give her these. I made them for her."

"Okay, okay," Pat grumbled as she reached for a homemade dog biscuit. Despite the fact that Tiki was just as content with the dog treats, Pat always seemed compelled to sneak her a regular cookie. "Anyway," she continued as Tiki happily crunched away, "I was at the store and ran into Gail Hunter. Are you sure I didn't tell you? I feel like I did. I can even remember thinking to myself at the time that I would have to tell you."

"I'm positive," I said, taking a cookie. "So, what happened?"

"Well, she looked awful," Pat said. "Like she hadn't slept in a week. Naturally, I asked her if she was okay and if she needed me to tell you to send her a package of Deep Sleep tea. She thanked me and said that wasn't necessary, as she already had some. But at that point, even your tea couldn't help.

"I asked why, and she told me that for the past few nights, she had been woken up in the dead of night by the sound of a horse galloping on the road. I couldn't believe it. Who would be riding a horse in the middle of the night? On a city street? She said she didn't know, because by the time she got to the window, there was nothing there."

"That's exactly how Wyle tells it," I said.

"I guess it's pretty creepy and disturbing to hear," Pat said. "And you know Gail. She's like you … has lived all her life in a haunted house. A little ghost isn't going to bother her. But this … this had her shaken." Pat shivered and took another bite of cookie.

Even though I was still sure the whole thing was some sort of prank, I was starting to feel a little disturbed, as well. "What about the jack-o'-lantern? Did she have one left in her yard?"

"On her front porch," Pat said. "It was right before the nightly horse galloping started. The whole experience has done a number on her. She told me she was considering taking off for a few weeks to go see her sister. She's getting to the point of not feeling safe in her own home."

I was flabbergasted. "She's THAT spooked?"

Pat nodded. "I know. It's weird, isn't it? The whole conversation was bizarre. That's why I'm sure I told you."

"Trust me, I would have remembered this story," I said.

Pat picked up her mug, but she didn't take a drink—merely cupped it in her hand, like she was trying to absorb the warmth. "I just don't know what to make of it. I've never heard of anything like this in Redemption."

"So, Redemption doesn't have its own version of the Headless Horseman?"

"Not that I've encountered." She sipped her tea, her face thoughtful. "So, if it isn't one of Redemption's legends, where DID it come from? Is it possible it followed this Ike person here?"

"You're assuming there's a real Headless Horseman in Sleepy Hollow," I said. "You do understand that the whole thing is a fiction story, right?"

Pat waved her hand. "Yes, yes. I know that. But lots of fiction stories are based on real events. Maybe this one is, too."

"Maybe," I said. "But doubtful. Especially since the Ichabod Crane in the story was never seen again."

"Well, maybe Ike should be careful," Pat said. "Stay away from all headless horsemen."

"That's probably good advice for all of us," I said. "That aside, my point is that if there WAS a real Headless Horseman after Ike, would Ike have turned up in Redemption? Or would he have already vanished?"

"Hmm," Pat said, tapping a finger to her lips. "Maybe that's what was fictionalized. Maybe Ichabod Crane didn't disappear after all."

"Yeah, maybe that whole experience inspired him to become a ghost hunter instead," I said.

"Exactly." Pat beamed "Now you're talking."

I shook my head bemusedly. "So, if all that was the case, I suppose it's possible the ghost of the Headless Horseman is following Ike around and wreaking havoc. But I always thought ghosts were linked to a location, not a person."

"Yeah, I guess that's what I always thought, too," Pat said. "But if that's the case, then where is this Headless Horseman coming from?"

"Well, first off, we don't know if it's the Headless Horseman," I said. "We don't even know if it's a ghost. It could be a prank."

Pat frowned. "Yeah, that's what I was assuming. But when I brought that up to Gail, she said she was sure it wasn't."

"Did she say why she's so sure?"

Pat shook her head. "No. It was clear she didn't want to talk about it. She was … I don't know if 'scared' is the right word. Maybe 'freaked out' is better."

I didn't know Gail well. She was a tea client and a fellow resident of a haunted house. But she had always struck me as down-to-earth and practical, nothing ever getting to her. The fact that this incident had gotten under her skin so much bothered me more than I wanted to admit.

"Why were you talking to Ike, anyway?" Pat asked suddenly. "And for that matter, Wyle?"

I paused to take a sip of tea. "Wyle wanted to meet for lunch," I said.

Pat raised an eyebrow. "Oh, did he now?"

"Stop it," I said. "It wasn't like that."

"Mmm hmm," Pat said. "No wonder you were so cagey when you started this story."

"I was so 'cagey,' as you put it …" I said, "because Wyle wanted to tell me about this jack-o'-lantern stuff and the horse galloping, as the occurrences seem to be targeting Redemption's haunted houses."

Pat stared at me, the subject of lunch with Wyle seemingly on the back burner. "Wait. You're telling me other haunted houses have been targeted, but not yours? The most haunted house in Redemption?"

"It seems that way," I said. Until Pat said it, it hadn't even occurred to me. "That is kind of weird, isn't it?"

"I would say so," Pat answered. "I wonder what it means, if anything."

"It's probably just a coincidence," I said, although I was becoming more and more apprehensive the more we talked. Maybe Gail leaving to visit her sister wasn't so far-fetched after all.

"So, you had a lunch date with Wyle ..." Pat circled back.

"It wasn't a date," I interrupted. "We were talking about a case."

"Of course you were," Pat said with a grin. "But that still doesn't explain how you met Ike."

I explained how Wyle was running late, so I sat in the bar, and after Ike spilled his beer all over, I ended up chatting with him.

Pat was watching me tell the story, a slight smile on her lips.

"Why are you looking at me like that?" I demanded.

She widened her eyes. "I'm not doing anything."

"Yes, you are," I grumbled. "Nothing happened today other than finding out that Redemption might have its own Headless Horseman creating chaos."

"Of course," Pat murmured, picking up her mug and taking a sip.

Argh. I couldn't wait for the day to be over.

Chapter 4

After parking on the side of the busy residential street where my tea client and fellow haunted-house owner Lee Rice lived, I double-checked behind me for cars before collecting my bag and her tea order and climbing out of the car.

Normally, I parked in the driveway, as Lee's street seemed to have way more traffic than most residential streets in Redemption. But there already was a car there—one I didn't recognize. Lee hadn't mentioned having any company, so I hoped dropping off her order wasn't a problem.

She had called me that morning, asking for a rush delivery of my Deep Sleep tea, as she was about to run out and didn't think she could make it through the night without it. I had already planned to make other deliveries anyhow, so I told her it wouldn't be an issue.

I avoided the overgrown yard and headed up the driveway to the large, rambling house. It very much looked haunted, with its broken-down shutters, sunken porch, and chipped paint. Ever since Lee's husband died a few years back, she hadn't been able to keep up with it, and it was slowly settling into a decrepit mess.

I carefully mounted the cracked porch steps, intentional about where I put my feet so I wouldn't trip, and rang the doorbell. I listened to it echo throughout the house before hearing footsteps coming toward me. The front door cracked open. "Charlie!" Lee's face was wreathed with a large smile as she held open the door. "Come in! I'm so glad you're here."

"Is this a bad time?" I asked as I stepped into the foyer. The house smelled of dust and neglect. A stack of mail was balanced precariously on a corner table, and the floor was clearly in need of a good sweeping.

Lee shook her head, her helmet of permed, tight curls barely moving. "Not at all. Why would you think that?" She blinked owlishly at me from behind thick glasses.

"There's a car in your driveway," I said.

Her face brightened again. "Oh! Of course. But that's part of why I'm so glad you're here. Come." She put a hand on my arm and led me to the old-fashioned kitchen, the floorboards squeaking beneath our steps. A man was sitting at the round, wooden table, his back to us.

"Here she is," Lee sang out as we entered. "She came by, just as I said she would."

The man turned, and I realized it was Ike. He flashed me a wide smile. "You sure did. So we meet again, Charlie."

"Uh, yes … hi, Ike," I greeted him.

Lee's brow wrinkled. "Oh, you two know each other."

"We've met," Ike said quickly, sending that same, wide smile to Lee. "But she left before I could get her number, so I'm so glad you're introducing her to me again."

Lee looked relieved. "I'm glad to help."

I glanced between the two of them, trying to figure out what was going on. Was this all a set-up to get me there? I held up the tea bag. "Does this mean you don't need the tea after all, or …?"

Lee's eyes widened. "Oh, heaven's no." She snatched the bag away from me. "I am SO grateful you brought it by today. Her Deep Sleep blend is fabulous," she said to Ike, who nodded. "I honestly couldn't sleep without it. Especially now."

My ears perked up at the "especially now" comment, but first, I wanted to clarify. "So, then … I don't understand," gesturing between the two of them. "You just told him I'd be here?" Addressing Ike, I said, "Were you trying to get me here, or something?"

Lee stared at me and then started to laugh. "Now I get it. Yes, I see why that would be confusing. No, it was all just serendipitous. Ike didn't show up until this afternoon, after I had already called you. But I admit, I was hoping you would arrive while he was here."

"I'm glad it worked out," I said faintly.

Lee patted my arm. "Sit, sit. I'll get you a cup of tea."

"Yes, please stay," Ike said as he pulled a chair out next to him.

Not sure how to say no, or if I even wanted to, I sat down. Lee bustled off into the kitchen. "So, how did I even come up in the conversation?"

"Oh, because we were talking about haunted houses," Lee called out as she dug a mug out of the cupboard. "Ike here is researching ghosts and haunted places in the Midwest, so of course, visiting Redemption was a must. And I told him your house should definitely be on his list."

"I see," I said, giving Ike a look. He shot me an innocent grin, holding his hands up like it wasn't his fault.

"It would be great to feature Helen's house in the book," Ike said. "It feels incomplete without it."

"It sure does," Lee piped in, carefully carrying the mug filled with a pale-brownish liquid toward me. I knew from experience the water would be tepid and the tea weak, but I smiled and took it anyway.

"I could see why you would think that," I said, keeping my response as neutral as possible. I had no intention of having my house featured in any book, but that was a discussion for another day. Lee certainly didn't need to be a part of it, especially since I could see how excited she was for her home to be highlighted in Ike's book. "But let's talk about why you need the tea," I said, changing the subject. "You said you were having trouble sleeping 'especially now.' Has something changed?"

Lee had been taking a sip of tea, but she put her mug down with a clatter. "Heavens yes. It's been horrible this past week, what with the horses and jack-o'-lanterns and all."

Next to me, Ike stilled. "Horses?" he asked, his voice cracking slightly.

Lee nodded and pushed her glasses up on her nose. "Such a racket," she said before patting my hand. "I just saw Gail in the grocery store the other day, and she was telling me it was so bad at her place, she was leaving town for a bit. How about you, dear?"

"So far, I've been lucky," I said. "I haven't been bothered."

"I'm so glad to hear that," she said, shaking her head slightly. "I wouldn't wish it on my worst enemy."

"What is … what's going on?" Ike asked. I could see he was rattled but trying to hide it. He picked up his mug, but his hand was trembling, and some tea sloshed over the side. I wondered why he was affected so much. Did he know something he wasn't sharing? Had Wyle had a chat with him?

Lee didn't seem to notice. "Someone has been putting jack-o'-lanterns on porches," Lee explained. "It's probably kids. That's what I told Gail, too, but she's just …" Lee shook her head.

"Jack-o'-lanterns?" Ike asked.

"Yes, it's very strange," Lee said. "I've had two show up so far. But that's not the worst part. Whoever is riding that poor horse at night is much worse."

Ike swallowed. "Horse?"

"Yes, there's a distinct, loud pounding of hooves on the pavement and neighing. It's been waking the whole neighborhood."

This seemed to drain the blood from Ike's face. His mouth moved, and I could have sworn I heard him mutter under his breath. "Not again."

Now, he really had my attention. "Did you say something?" I asked Ike.

He shook his head violently. "No … no. How long has this been happening?"

"Just twice in the past few days. It's just …" Lee shivered. "It's creepy. It doesn't last long, and by the time you get to the window to look out, there's nothing there."

Ike offered a strained smile and pushed his mug around in circles. "You know, I'm so sorry, but I just realized I need to go. Raincheck?"

"Oh!" Lee was visibly flustered. "But I haven't given you a tour yet. And we haven't finished the interview."

"I'll be in touch, I promise," he said, rising to his feet and waving at Lee to stay where she was. Then, he met my eyes. "I guess it's my turn to run. I'm so sorry, Charlie. I would love to pick this chat up another time?"

"Of course," I said, my brain whirling. What could cause him to leave so suddenly? Did he know something about the jack-o'-lanterns and horse galloping after all?

He nodded to both of us and quickly headed out of the kitchen and front door.

"Mercy," Lee said after the door closed. "That was very strange. Do you think it was something we said?"

"I don't see how it could be," I reassured her. "He's a ghost hunter, after all. If a few jack-o'-lanterns and the sound of a horse galloping can scare him off, he can't be a very good one, can he?"

"I suppose you're right," Lee said, picking up her mug. But her expression was skeptical.

I didn't blame her. I was feeling skeptical myself. Especially since I was sure if Ike wasn't outright lying, there was definitely something he wasn't telling us.

Chapter 5

"He actually said 'not again'?" Pat's eyes were wide as she stared at me.

"That's what it sounded like," I said. "But he muttered it under his breath. I wouldn't swear to it in a court of law."

After leaving Lee's house, I ended up going to Pat's. I couldn't stop thinking about what I was sure I'd heard, and I wanted to talk to someone about it. A part of me wanted to find Wyle, but I wasn't quite ready yet.

I hadn't spoken to him since our strange and abruptly aborted lunch experience. Nor had I decided how I felt about it. On one hand, it was exactly what I expected. We met for lunch and chatted about a case. Period. It was not a date, nor had he set it up as one. So, it exactly matched the expectation. Nothing more, nothing less.

So why did I feel so oddly let down by it?

It wasn't like I could date Wyle even if I wanted to. My history was way too complicated to date anyone, much less a cop. So, there was really no good reason for what I was feeling.

Yet none of that seemed to make any difference in how I felt. Nor did it inspire me to want to see him again.

Needless to say, I knew it was also a childish attitude to have. Pat was right. I should tell Wyle what I thought Ike said. Because if Ike WAS behind the pranks, or if he knew who was, Wyle would want to put a stop to it.

"Still, you should do something," Pat said. "*We* should do something."

"What do you think we should do?"

We were sitting in Pat's spotless kitchen. She was a bit of a neat freak, so if she wasn't helping me with a case or involved in one of her endless volunteer projects, she was likely cleaning her house. The only reason she had even agreed to take Tiki in was because she was a toy poodle, and therefore didn't shed.

Speaking of Tiki, she was happily perched on my lap, wearing a bright-blue sweater with matching blue ribbons. Even though she clearly loved Pat to pieces, she had a soft spot for me in her heart, as I had helped her out of an unpleasant situation in one of my recent cases.

"Well, tell Wyle, for one," Pat said. "I'm assuming you did that."

I decided that Tiki needed a good neck scratch, right under her collar. She stretched her neck out in response, obviously agreeing with me.

"Well?" Pat asked, raising an eyebrow. "Charlie, you did tell him, right?"

"I thought I'd start with you," I admitted.

Pat gave me an exasperated look. "Me? Why would you start with me? Not that I don't appreciate being first to know, but it's not like I can dig around in Ike's history."

"I know, I know," I said with a sigh. "You're right, I need to go talk to him."

Pat's eyes narrowed. "Is this because of that lunch? I thought you said it wasn't a date."

"It *wasn't* a date," I said.

"Then why are you pouting?"

"I'm NOT pouting," I insisted.

"What exactly do you call it, then?"

"I …" I glowered at her. "I don't know. I haven't been myself lately. I don't know why."

Pat gave me a knowing look. "I do," she said. "It probably has to do with a disappointing date."

"It has nothing to do with that," I said. "I'm probably on edge because Halloween is a bad time to be in Redemption. All the ghosts are restless. And this whole jack-o'-lantern, horse-galloping-around-Redemption's-haunted-houses stuff is bothering me. I feel like I'm on pins and needles just waiting for my turn. And why *hasn't* my turn come? That's bothersome, too."

"Yeah, I get that," Pat said. "The energy is always off in Redemption during October. You're probably right. That's all this is." She gave me an innocent smile, which made me grit my teeth. Ugh. She knew me too well.

"Okay, I guess I better go see Wyle," I said, getting up and handing Tiki to Pat. "Do you want to come, too?"

"You better believe it," Pat said. "Someone needs to chaperone."

* * *

"He actually said 'not again'?" Wyle asked, a note of disbelief in his voice. I felt like I was experiencing Déjà vu.

We were in the police station, Pat and I sitting across from Wyle's very messy desk. Piles of paper were balanced precariously on the surface, and every time I came in, I wondered if that would be the day I would see one of them finally tip over and spill onto the gray linoleum floor.

"He said it under his breath," I said. "I can't be 100 percent sure. But yeah, that's what it sounded like. Plus, he looked like he saw a ghost."

"A ghost," Wyle repeated, fishing around his desk for a pen. I held my breath, waiting for a stack to fall, but alas, they somehow defied gravity and stayed put. "Like a Headless Horseman type of ghost?"

"Maybe," I said. "I didn't ask."

Even though Redemption was a small town, the police station always seemed to be bustling with activity no matter when I arrived, and it was no different then. Around me, I could hear the clatter of the typewriter as one of the officers pecked away at a form along with a constant stream of voices talking and phones ringing. The air was filled with the smell of old, burnt coffee, stale sweat, and old socks. I always found myself trying to hold my breath or breathe through my mouth in that building.

"I didn't think you believe in ghosts," Pat piped in. "Or in this case, the Headless Horseman."

"I try to keep an open mind," Wyle said, jotting down a few notes. "Especially when we keep getting calls about late-night horse galloping."

"So, that's still going on?" I asked.

He nodded as he glanced up, eying me from over the stacks of paper. "I take it you haven't had any issues yet."

I raised an eyebrow. "Yet? You're assuming I will?"

Wyle started pawing through his desk again. "I think I've heard from nearly every haunted house or building or whatever in this town. So, yes, I think you'll get your turn eventually. The real question is, why haven't you yet?"

"That *is* puzzling," Pat said.

I made a face at her. "Maybe the haunted part is just a co-incidence."

Wyle's expression was skeptical. "Seriously? A coincidence?"

"Well, it's not like Redemption is lacking in haunted build-ings," I said. "Heavens, you can practically throw a rock and hit something that someone swears is haunted. What if just seems like it's connected to haunted houses, but it's really just ran-dom?"

I wasn't sure if I completely bought that explanation myself, as the fact that nothing had happened to me yet bothered me more than I wanted to admit. Not that I wanted anything to happen, of course. But why would I be spared?

Unless I wasn't being spared at all. Maybe I was being saved for something special … something even worse.

"Maybe," Wyle said, not sounding particularly convinced.

"It would explain why I haven't heard anything, anyway," I said. "I'm out in the middle of nowhere, as you keep pointing out. Why would anyone waste a good scare in the middle of nowhere?"

Wyle tapped his pen on his notebook, a peculiar look on his face. "Maybe you're not getting pranked because whoever is behind it has a soft spot for you."

"What?" I was sure I didn't hear him right. "Who do you think has a soft spot for me?"

Wyle gave me another look. "Who do you think?"

"If you're talking about Ike, I can assure you he doesn't have a 'soft spot' or anything remotely like that for me," I said, my tone haughty.

"Then why is it you just happen to keep running into him?"

"I haven't a clue, but it's probably nothing more than coincidence," I said.

"I don't believe in coincidence," Wyle muttered.

"It could be Redemption," Pat piped in. I had forgotten she was there. Both Wyle and I snapped our heads around to stare at her. Pat saw our expressions and seemed to shrink back into her chair. "Well, we all know Redemption has its own ideas about what should happen in this town."

"Great. Redemption is playing matchmaker now," Wyle said, his tone disgusted.

"There IS no matchmaking going on," I insisted. "I happened to run into him twice. That's it. Redemption is a small town. It's not that unusual."

"Uh huh," Wyle said. "What about finagling an invitation for drinks or dinner? Is that also 'not that unusual'?"

I could feel my cheeks flush. "It's not like that," I said. "He wants to research my house."

"Oh. 'Research.' Is that what he's calling it?"

"What, are you jealous or something? I live in a haunted house, and he is doing research on haunted houses. In fact, I found him sitting at the kitchen table in Lee Rice's house! Is he asking her out, too?"

A cold, wet nose pressed against my forearm. I looked down to see Tiki's bright little black eyes looking up at me. I suddenly realized my voice had been getting louder and louder, and other officers and visitors were starting to notice.

Wyle also seemed to have realized we were becoming the center of attention in the station. He made a point of straightening his notebook and jotting something down, although I had a feeling it was probably nonsense. "Anything else to report?"

I took a deep breath and smoothed my sweater. "No, I think that's enough."

Wyle made a sound somewhere between a yelp and a laugh. "Enough? No, enough would be telling Ike to come in and answer some questions. Or better yet, maybe calling me when you're with him to see if I could get there in time to talk to him."

"If you want my help, you could just ask," I said. "Are you saying you haven't talked to him yet? I had no idea. I assumed you already interviewed him."

Wyle shifted uncomfortably in his seat, as if suddenly realizing how he sounded. "He hasn't responded to my messages yet," he said stiffly.

There was an awkward silence. "I guess if I run into him again, I can let him know you'd like to talk," I said. "I don't know how effective that would be, but I could try."

Wyle opened his mouth and shut it, as if changing his mind about what he was going to say. "I would appreciate it," he said.

There was another awkward silence. "Well, I guess that covers it," Pat interjected brightly, getting to her feet. "Unfortunately, Charlie and I need to be going. You'll keep us posted on any new developments, right Wyle?"

"Of course," Wyle said. He had smoothed his expression over, and his voice was back to neutral. "Just like I trust you'll do the same." He directed that sentence at me, and I could just hear the threat underneath the bland tone.

"I always do," I threw back, standing up to follow Pat out of the station.

"That was fun," Pat said under her breath as we headed out of the station. "You know, it would probably make things so much easier if you two would just go out on an actual date already."

"I'm NOT dating Wyle," I said, gritting my teeth. "I have no interest in dating anyone … and certainly not him."

Both Pat and Tiki eyed me with a knowing look. "Of course not," Pat said.

Chapter 6

A couple of days later, I was heading down Main Street to deliver a tea order when I caught sight of Ike.

I had nearly convinced myself I wasn't going to see him again, which suited me just fine. There was no question that not seeing him would make my life so much easier. I had no desire to have any sort of relationship with him, not to mention have my house mentioned in any sort of publication. Just the thought of people lined up outside wanting some sort of tour made me break out in cold sweats. Absolutely not.

Nor was I the least bit interested in becoming Wyle's errand girl. Did he really expect me to tell Ike he needed to go answer a few questions from the police? How was that my problem? If Wyle wanted to interview Ike, he could do his own dirty work, thank you very much.

As far as I was concerned, if I never saw Ike again, that would be too soon. It seemed like one complication after another since the day I decided to help him salvage his papers from his spilled beer, and I was tired of it. I put him firmly out of my mind and went back to focusing on my tea business. Out of sight, out of mind.

At least, that was my hope.

It was a beautiful autumn day. The sun was out, and the air was just a bit nippy, just enough to require my jean jacket. Scents of autumn wafted on the breeze—dried leaves and decaying plants, with a little bite that all but promised the cold of winter was on its way.

As I strolled by Quote the Raven, a huge new-and-used bookstore, I glanced up and happened to see Ike standing by the big glass window, paging through a book. A lock of brown hair fell over his forehead as he studied the contents.

Having convinced myself there was no way I was going to run into him again, it was a shock to see him there, and I ended up pausing mid-step. I even started to lift my hand to wave to him, my manners automatically kicking in, but at that very moment, the sun dipped behind a cloud, and a chill ran over my skin. I shivered, my thoughts going to a Headless Horseman galloping the dark streets, searching for his next victim …

I dropped my hand instinctively. What was I thinking? From the moment I met him, it had been one issue after another. Why on Earth would I be *waving* at him? I should be thankful I hadn't gotten his attention.

I was too late. Ike lifted his gaze from his book and looked directly into my eyes. Before I could move, his face broke into a smile, and he started waving frantically at me.

I waved back, not knowing what else to do. He dropped the book he was holding on a little table and ran to the front door to open it.

"Charlie," he called out. "I was hoping to run into you. Do you have a minute?"

Before I could answer, the sun burst from behind the clouds, its cheerful rays making everything feel so much warmer and inviting. It felt like a sign. Plus, my innate curiosity was getting the better of me, despite knowing that chances were high this was just a ploy to get me to say yes to him researching my house. But just in case it wasn't …

"Sure," I answered, trying not to think about Wyle's reaction. Ike grinned and held the door open for me, making it easier for me to duck inside.

The bookstore had that papery smell I loved. I took a deep breath, inhaling it, and immediately felt more relaxed.

"Wow, this is turning into such a great day," Ike said. "My luck is definitely shifting for the better."

"Because you ran into me?" I asked. I wasn't sure if he was flirting with me or just buttering me up for his ask.

His grin widened. "Absolutely. You're the second-best thing to happen to me today."

Second? I could feel my ego deflate. So much for flirting. "What was the first?"

"This." He picked up the book he had been reading and showed it to me. "Check out this find."

I glanced at the cover, which looked a bit amateurish—*The True History of Redemption: Fact and Fiction*. "I haven't heard of it."

"I'm not surprised," Ike said, tucking the book under his arm. "It's self-published by one of Redemption's top historians. I'm stoked I was able to locate a copy."

"I didn't know there was a top historian for Redemption," I said.

"There's always a top historian," Ike said. "Sometimes, you have to do a little digging to find him or her, is all. Speaking of digging, I have a question for you about your house. But first, I want to apologize for the other day."

"Why are you apologizing?" With any luck, it would be because he wasn't able to include my house in his book after all.

He sighed and ran his hand through his hair. "My reaction. The way I ran out on you and Lee."

I raised an eyebrow. This was promising. Maybe I would be able to get to the bottom of one mystery, at least, which would be a good start. "I thought you had to be somewhere. You didn't?"

His expression was sheepish. "No. I was just ..." He paused, looking like he was fighting within himself.

Now I was really intrigued. "What?"

He glanced around the bookstore, as if checking to see if anyone was eavesdropping before taking a step closer to me. "I think I'm being haunted," he said, lowering his voice.

"You're being ... haunted?" Pat's words about the Headless Horseman following Ike floated through my head. Was that where this was going? Maybe Wyle was right, and this was all a publicity stunt after all.

He nodded, his expression serious.

"By what?" A part of me couldn't believe he would say it. It was too obvious. Not to mention ridiculous.

He chewed on his lip for a moment before leaning even closer. "By the Headless Horseman."

For a moment, I only stared at him. Then, I began to laugh. "You really had me going," I said between chuckles.

Ike continued to stare at me, and I realized his expression was deadly serious. "Wait. You're not joking?"

"I wish I was," he said mournfully.

"You can't … but that's just a story," I said. "A made-up story. It's not true." But even as I said it, Ike's horrified expression and his muttered "not again" flashed through my mind. Did this mean he wasn't as skeptical as he first claimed?

"Irving didn't make up the Headless Horseman," Ike said. "There have been myths and stories about him for hundreds of years. Most of Western Europe has its own version of a Headless Horseman."

"Yes, but we're still talking about a ghost, right?"

"Not always," Ike said. "In Ireland, it's believed to be a demonic fairy."

"A demonic …" I couldn't even finish the sentence. I gave my head a quick shake. "I guess it's a good thing we're not in Ireland. But that aside, how is it you're being haunted by a ghost? I thought ghosts haunted places, not people. Wouldn't you be possessed rather than haunted?"

He raised his hands helplessly. "It's the only thing that makes any sense."

"Let's start from the beginning," I said. "*Why* do you think you're being haunted by the Headless Horseman? Because you're from Sleepy Hollow and your name is Ichabod Krane?"

He let out a snort. "I wish. No, what I told you earlier was true. I was a skeptic for most of my life, and part of the reason I became a ghost hunter was to debunk paranormal sightings."

"So what changed?"

He looked down, his body tense. "You're going to think I'm nuts."

"I live in Redemption," I said. "Trust me when I say I've heard many, many things that most people would consider nuts. Try me."

He flashed me a small smile. "Okay, well here goes. What would you say if I told you that Redemption isn't the first town I've visited where jack-o'-lanterns mysteriously appear on people's porches, and the sound of a horse galloping on the streets at night wakes people from their sleep?"

"You mean ... this has happened before?"

He slowly nodded.

"How many times?"

"Nearly every town I've been to for the past three months."

I stared at him. "Seriously?"

He nodded again. "At first, I thought it was a joke. Someone figured out my name and where I'm from and decided to pull a prank on me. But then, it kept happening. Over and over. I can't figure it out."

"What did you do about it?"

He held up his hands. "What could I? I need the research. My publisher is expecting the book. So, I tried keeping a low profile, even staying at a hotel outside of town. But it didn't matter. No matter where I went, the jack-o'-lanterns and sounds of the galloping horse continued to follow me."

"What about when you leave? Does it continue then?"

"No. It stops." He ran his hand through his hair again, causing tufts to stand up. "I followed up with several homeowners who had told me about these occurrences after I left, and they all said the same thing. As soon as I leave, those things stop happening. But then they start up in the new place I'm in."

"So you think the Headless Horseman is ... following you from town to town? Doing these things to the people you're interviewing?"

"Do you have a better explanation?"

"Well, I think the prank explanation is worth digging into," I said.

He gave me a look. "That's not even possible. You're saying there are people in every single town I've been to who know my name and where I'm from who have decided to pull the exact same prank?"

"That does sound a little improbable," I admitted. "But no more improbable than a Headless Horseman trailing across the country after you."

"I agree. The Headless Horseman theory does sound nuts," he said. "Believe me, I've spent hours and hours trying to come up with a different explanation. But nothing else makes sense."

"Have you tried investigating these claims?" I asked. "As a ghost hunter?"

He sighed. "I have. But the problem is, they don't happen when I'm actually in the area. It's like whatever it is knows where I am, so I've never personally experienced it."

"So, it's all hearsay?"

He nodded and raked his hand through his hair again. "Normally, if I'm not able to experience something firsthand, that's a big sign it's a sham. But this? All these people in completely different towns who don't know each other at all having the exact same story?" He shook his head. "I can't explain it."

"It does seem to defy explanation," I said. "And unfortunately, I can't help you, as I've been lucky enough to not have experienced it."

"Oh." Ike snapped his fingers. "That reminds me. I wanted to ask you, are you renting Helen Blackstone's house?"

"What? No." I stared at him, perplexed. "Why would you think that?"

"Because I finally found my notes, and it looks like Helen Blackstone's house is owned by a trust. That's one of the reasons I never reached out initially. I had planned to swing by while I was here, but assumed it was either vacant, or some company was managing it."

"Oh, that's my trust," I said. It had never occurred to me that my trust would be listed as owning the deed to the house, but it made sense. My family was wealthy enough that I had a trust fund—not enough to live on without ever working again, but enough to pay my mortgage each month, which gave me the security to start my tea and tincture business.

He blinked at me. "You have a trust?"

I flashed him a self-conscious smile. "It's not really something I like to talk about. I'm not terribly ... close with my family."

His eyes widened. "Oh. I'm sorry to hear that."

I waved my hand. "It's not a big deal. Honestly. Don't worry about it."

"Okay," he said, but he didn't look convinced. I wondered if what I said had touched a nerve. Maybe he wasn't close with his family, either. "So, the Blackstone house is truly yours?"

"It is."

He cocked his head and flashed a crooked grin that made me catch my breath. He really was good-looking. "So, what do I need to do to get an invitation? I promise I'll be on my best behavior." He pressed a hand to his chest. "Scout's honor. I only want to research the ghosts."

I smiled despite myself. "It's not that. I don't question your motives."

His smile faded. "Wait ... you're saying no?"

I held up my hands. "I don't want the publicity. You under-stand, right?"

He stared at me, flummoxed. "You honestly won't let me research your house?" His voice was shocked, like he had never been turned down before. With that charming smile, I had no doubt he probably hadn't heard the word "no" many times in his life.

"I'm afraid not," I said. "But the beauty of Redemption is that there are so many haunted places to check out. I assure you, you're not going to run out of places to research."

"Yes, but ..." He seemed completely at a loss for words. "Your house is considered the *most* haunted. It's like I said be-fore ... the book would be incomplete without the Blackstone house."

"I'm sure it will be fine," I said.

He gazed at me like he still couldn't believe I was actually turning him down. "There's nothing I can do to convince you otherwise?"

I shook my head. "'Fraid not. But I'm happy to help you in other ways. If you have questions or want me to introduce you to other people in town, I'd be glad to do that."

He was silent as he continued to study me. I couldn't read the expression on his face and wondered if he was about to give me a "Thanks, but no thanks."

"You're something else, Charlie," he finally said.

"I like to think so," I replied lightheartedly.

A ghost of a smile touched his lips. "Okay, then. I guess I'll take what I can get." He put down the book and started to rifle through a leather satchel he wore at his side. "Maybe I can get your help with some of my notes. Especially since I've been trying to keep my research time as short as possible." A cloud passed over his face, dulling his enthusiasm. "I don't want to … overstay my welcome."

His expression had turned brooding, and I assumed he was thinking about the supposed Headless Horseman following him around. "I get it," I said with a small smile, hoping to pull him out of his funk. "And I'd be happy to."

He took a deep breath, gave himself a quick shake, and started pulling out a large sheath of papers from his satchel. Almost as quickly, he seemed to think better of it and tucked them back in. "Actually, I have a lot of questions," he said, glancing up at me with that self-conscious grin. "It might take a while. Probably be better if we were sitting down somewhere. Maybe I can buy you a drink or meal?"

I eyed him. "You wouldn't be trying to bribe me in hopes of changing my mind about researching my house, would you?"

He widened his eyes in mock innocence and pressed a hand to his chest. "Heavens no. I wouldn't dream of it."

I pretended to mull it over. "Well, okay. If you're sure."

"Positive," he said, but his voice trailed off as his eyes shifted to the side of me. As I watched, his face drained of color again, taking on an almost chalky appearance.

"Ike? Are you okay?" I took a step forward, wondering if he was about to have a heart attack.

He didn't immediately answer—just stood there, frozen. I turned my head to see if there was anything going on that would cause such a reaction. Perhaps an accident, or one of Redemption's restless ghosts.

Or maybe the Headless Horseman was finally making an appearance.

A shiver crawled down my spine, and I pushed that thought away, which was easier to do when I looked outside at the bright, sunny day. As far as I could see, it appeared to be a perfectly normal fall day in downtown Redemption. People were out enjoying the weather, leisurely gazing into shops.

I turned back to Ike, saying his name again and taking another step toward him, sure he was having some sort of medical emergency. That seemed to jar him out of his daze. He blinked a couple of times before refocusing his gaze on me. "Sorry," he said. "I just ..." he cleared his throat. "Rain check? I just realized there's an important call I have to make."

"Of course," I said.

He gave me a watery smile. "Sorry ... I'm not normally so scattered, but sometimes when I'm traveling, I get my times mixed up. And I do have to make this call." He started to back away.

"I get it," I said. "We can definitely meet another time. Just let me know."

He was still backing away, but he nodded at me, his eyes shifting from side to side as if he were trying to look everywhere at once. "I'll call you," he called out before disappearing into the shelves of books.

"Okay," I said, although I didn't think he could hear me. I looked around, wondering why he hadn't gone through the front door instead of heading toward the back of the bookstore.

Was he going to use the bookstore's phone? I supposed that was a possibility. But something about it felt off.

I glanced out the window again, wondering if he had seen something after all. He had looked so pale, and his eyes had that fearful, hunted look I had become all too familiar with when I was running from my abusive fiancé. Maybe the Headless Horseman had been out there searching for him after all …

I gave my head a quick shake, telling myself firmly to stop with the Headless Horseman nonsense. Especially since I could see nothing out of the ordinary through the window … other than the fact that the bookstore faced a shop called "Psychic Readings by Madame Rowena." Worse, I could see Madame Rowena standing in her doorway looking straight at me. She was dressed in her normal long, silk, beaded clothes, with a sparkling golden scarf twisted around her head.

I gritted my teeth. I was not a fan of Madame Rowena, nor was she of me. Not only was I convinced she was a fake, but I also had a sneaking suspicion she was doing everything in her power to turn the people in Redemption against me.

Our eyes met, and she flashed me a cold smile. I wondered how long she had been standing there. Had she seen me talking to Ike? The thought made me uncomfortable, although I couldn't put a finger on why. There was nothing going on between Ike and me, so why would it matter if she saw us together?

Still, it niggled at me.

I broke eye contact first. I was being ridiculous. Plus, I had better things to do than stand around in the middle of a bookstore. I had tea deliveries to make. As I turned to leave, my eyes caught sight of the book Ike had been so excited about. He was in such a rush to leave, he'd left it behind.

I picked it up, remembering how his face lit up as he showed it to me. That must have been some phone call he needed to make for him to forget about it.

Unless … it wasn't a phone call after all.

In my mind, I could almost hear the sounds of a horse galloping on the city streets, a loud neigh breaking the stillness, and see a jack-o'-lantern on my porch step ...

Even though I knew it was absurd on so many levels, I couldn't push the thoughts out of my head. Redemption was a strange, haunted town. Would it be *that* odd for the Headless Horseman to show up?

Especially if it was following Ike, named after its adversary, around the country?

Giving my head another quick shake, I carried the book to the middle of the store where the cash register was. A high-school-aged girl was behind the counter, reading a book. Her mousy brown hair was tucked behind her ears, and she wore tortoise- shell glasses.

She looked up rather reluctantly as I approached. "Can I help you?"

I held up the book. "My friend wanted to buy this, but he had to leave for an emergency. Would you mind holding it for him?"

She looked at the book but didn't take it. "I can only hold it until closing time today. After that, it goes back on the shelf."

"Oh." I paused, still holding it, thinking about my options. I had no way of getting ahold of Ike, so I wouldn't be able to tell him he had to come back before closing time if he wanted it. Although I had to wonder ... would something this obscure be in that much demand?

"Maybe I should just buy it for him," I said.

"You could do that," the girl agreed.

"Maybe you saw him?" I asked. "He said he had to make an important phone call."

"Oh, yes. Him," she said, gesturing toward the back. "We have a payphone back there. It's through the door and next to the bathrooms."

"Perfect," I said. "Let me go see if he's still there."

She nodded and went back to her book as I headed to the back of the bookstore.

I ducked through the door and found myself in a dusty hallway. On one side were two bathrooms with a water fountain and payphone in the middle, but there was no Ike.

Puzzled, I walked around, wondering if he was in the bathroom. I took a quick peek down the hall and found a couple of closed doors, one labeled "Exit."

Could Ike have left?

I went back and studied the door to the men's room, wondering if it was worth it to check. I waited for a few minutes before tapping on the door and pushing it open a few inches—not enough to see in. "Ike," I called out. "Are you in there?"

No answer.

Puzzled, I went back to the cashier, who again begrudgingly dragged her eyes away from her book. "Was he there?"

"No. I didn't see him."

Her expression didn't change. "Oh. Well, does that mean you want to buy the book or not?"

I tilted my head. "You don't find it strange he wasn't back there?"

She shrugged. "Not really. There's an exit there, too. It goes out to a back alley."

I was surprised at her nonchalance. "Can people get in from that exit?"

"No, it locks from the outside. Are you going to buy it, or not?"

I looked down at the book again. A part of me was insisting I had no business getting involved, and I should hand the book to the cashier and be on my way.

But another part of me told that part to zip it.

"Let me see if I have enough cash," I said, reaching for my wallet.

Chapter 7

"Yes, Ike Krane is staying here," Nancy said, tucking a hunk of brittle, over-permed, over-colored hair behind one ear as she replaced the empty coffee pot with a full one. Her silver-rimmed glasses swung on a chain across her blouse. "Popular guy. Is he famous or something?"

Nancy, who owned the Redemption Inn, was not only my friend, but also my first tea customer. She helped spread the word about my fledging tea and tincture business, recommending my blends to people like Pat.

"As far as I know, he's not famous," I said. "He's an author and ghost hunter."

"A ghost hunter! He'll have plenty to keep him busy in this town then," Nancy said with a laugh as she moved on from the coffee to arranging a platter of freshly baked gingersnaps. I caught a whiff of them and could hear my stomach grumble. As much as I thought my homemade cookies were the best in town, Nancy's famous gingersnaps were the one exception.

Nancy must have read it on my face, as she reached over to hand me a cookie and napkin.

"I shouldn't," I said as I took it.

"Of course you should," she said with a wink.

We were standing in the front of her hotel next to the built-in counter where she kept a never-ending pot of coffee and usually some sort of baked treats, as well. On one side was the check-in desk, and behind us was the huge lobby filled with overstuffed chairs, couches, and a massive fireplace that was wonderful to snuggle up to when winter hit. Even though there wasn't currently a fire, a number of guests were hanging out reading or chatting. One woman with long, dark hair was sitting by herself in the corner doing a crossword puzzle in a newspaper.

I hadn't been able to stop thinking about Ike and his bizarre story. He couldn't really believe that there was really a Headless Horseman, right? It had to be a big publicity stunt. Although, I had to admit, it was brilliant. All of these towns talking about how they had been visited by the Headless Horseman because of Ike. He would probably end up with a bestseller on his hands.

The problem with that theory was that Ike truly seemed terrified. Was it possible he was that good of an actor? Something inside me didn't think so, but I couldn't rule it out.

I also knew I should find Wyle and fill him in on what happened. He should know that Ike was claiming these pranks— or whatever they were—had been happening in other towns. Maybe he could even call some of them and verify precisely what was going on.

Even though I knew I should tell Wyle, a part of me didn't want to. I was dreading the conversation we were sure to have, especially since I hadn't had the opening to encourage Ike to reach out to Wyle. Ugh. I just knew that would make Wyle accuse me of something. I didn't know what his problem was, but he was driving me crazy.

I ended up taking my own sweet time with my tea deliveries, chatting with my clients to make sure all was well in their world and asking if there was anything else I could help them with. I told myself I was being a good businesswoman—that it had nothing to do with wasting time so I would have an excuse to avoid the police station. If it was close to five, I was sure Wyle wouldn't want to see me anyhow. He would want to wait until tomorrow.

After finishing the deliveries, I leisurely strolled back to my car and realized that I hadn't parked all that far away from the Redemption Inn. As I still had the book Ike wanted tucked away in my purse, I thought it would be foolish to not stop by and see if he was staying there. He had been so excited to find the book, I was sure he would want it as soon as possible.

"Is he investigating your house? Is that why you're trying to find him?" Nancy asked, wiping a few crumbs off the counter.

"Not exactly," I said. "Who else is looking for him?"

"Well, Wyle for one," Nancy said. "Does Wyle need the services of a ghost hunter?"

"I wouldn't be surprised," I said. "It's Redemption, after all."

"Not to mention Halloween is coming, which is always a busy time here," Nancy said as she picked up the empty coffee pot to take into the kitchen located in the back. "Did you want to leave a message for Ike?" she asked over her shoulder.

A surge of disappointment shot through me. "He's not here?"

"I don't think so," she said. "But I can try his room. Give me a minute." She disappeared into the kitchen. I waited by the desk for her to reappear, adjusting her reading glasses on her nose. She paged through her reservation book for a moment before picking up the phone and punching in a number. She glanced at me as she listened to it ring. "He doesn't seem to be in," she said.

"You didn't seem to expect him to be ... is there a reason why?" I asked.

"Because I saw him a while ago," Nancy said, replacing the receiver. "He flew in like a bat out of hell and went straight to his room. I was wondering if he was unwell or something. I haven't seen anyone move that fast in ages. And about ten minutes later, he ran back through again." She made a gesture with her hand, as if tracing his path. "All I could think was he must have been late for something."

"Excuse me." The dark-haired woman was standing behind me. She was pretty, in a delicate sort of way, with large brown eyes and a heart-shaped face. She stammered when I turned around, dropping her eyes to the floor while a faint blush stained her cheeks. "Did I hear you mention Ike Krane?"

"Yes ... who are you?" I asked.

"Another person who was asking about Ike," Nancy chimed in.

The woman's blush deepened. I gave Nancy a look. "Don't mind her. How do you know Ike?"

"I'm Kat, Ike's girlfriend," she said, her voice soft.

Nancy's eyebrows went up. "Oh. You didn't tell me you were his girlfriend," she said.

Kat was still staring at the floor, although one slender hand had started twisting a long lock of hair. "It's … complicated. Can we talk for a minute?" she asked me.

I nodded, feeling even more curious about the enigma that was Ike. Especially when I thought about the flirtatious look in his eyes when he asked me to join him for a drink or meal. Although maybe that wasn't all that surprising. He certainly wouldn't be the first man to decide to have a little fun when the girlfriend wasn't around.

She led me across the polished hardwood floor back to the corner where she had been sitting. The folded newspaper was still on the table next to a pen. I was impressed she had been doing the crossword in ink.

She sat down in the same seat she had been in, leaving me to settle into the chair in front of her, my back to the lobby and facing the log-cabin wall covered with a brightly colored quilt. I shifted a little uncomfortably, at a disadvantage if Ike were to run back through again. Although it was possible that was the point. Kat wouldn't be the first woman to suspect her boyfriend of having a little on the side when she wasn't around, either, and it was possible she was suspicious of any woman who was tracking Ike down.

Kat pulled the newspaper toward her and started worrying the corner. "Have you met Ike?" Her long hair fell across her shoulders, obscuring part of her face.

"Yes, a few days ago," I said, placing the cookie and napkin on the table.

"Are you part of his research?"

"Not exactly," I said. "He spilled his beer over his notes. I helped him out, and we ended up chatting a bit."

A small smile touched her lips. "That's so Ike. He is such a klutz."

"Yeah, he does seem a little clumsy," I said.

She continued worrying the edge of her newspaper. "Have you seen him since?"

There was something about her that didn't sit right with me, although I couldn't put my finger on it. "Yes, he wanted to interview me about all the different hauntings in Redemption." I figured that was true enough for the moment.

She seemed to visibly relax at that, her shoulders relaxing and the air leaving her chest. "Of course. That makes perfect sense. I should have trusted him." Her voice was so quiet, I almost didn't hear her.

"I'm sorry?"

She gave her head a quick shake, a few pieces of hair flying around her head like a cloud. "It's just … I wasn't exactly honest with you," she said.

"Oh?"

She blushed again. "It's just … I'm not currently his girlfriend. We, uh …" she sighed. "We broke up."

"Ah." Now Ike's flirtation made more sense. I tried to bury how relieved I felt that he wasn't a cheater.

She peeked at me through the curtain of her hair. Something flitted across her face, so fast I couldn't read it, and almost immediately, she lowered her head again. "It's my fault. I messed everything up."

"That's tough," I said sympathetically. "Maybe Ike will give you another chance."

She sighed. "Hopefully. But I don't know …" Her voice drifted off, and she refocused on the corner of the newspaper. I got the feeling she wanted to talk to someone.

"I know it's none of my business, but if you want to talk, I'm a good listener," I offered.

She peeked at me from behind her hair, and a faint smile touching her lips. "I appreciate that. It's been really difficult."

"I bet."

"You see, I was … with someone when Ike and I first met."

"Ah," I said. I had misread the situation. It wasn't Ike being unfaithful. It was Kat.

She blushed. "It's not what you think," she said. "About a year ago, I moved to Sleepy Hollow with my fiancé, Abe. Abe had gotten transferred in his company. I got a job at one of the school districts. I'm a teacher. That's where I met Ike."

"Ike is a teacher?" I was surprised. I had assumed his career focus was ghost hunting and writing.

She grinned, the first real smile I had seen from her. "Despite what you might have heard, ghost hunting alone doesn't pay the bills. His writing helps some, but he needs a steady income. Not to mention benefits. So, being a substitute teacher helped fill in the gaps. It gave him some flexibility to pursue his other interests while keeping him financially stable."

"That makes sense," I said. I wondered how he was able to balance being a substitute teacher with traveling to all these different cities for his book research.

She must have followed my train of thought. "He's not working as a substitute teacher now."

"He's not?"

She shook her head, biting her lip like she was trying to keep herself from crying. "No, he quit. Because of me and my screwup."

"What happened?" I asked, keeping my voice gentle.

She looked down, her hair falling in front of her face again. "Abe was … well, I guess I'll just say it. He was abusive."

"Oh." I jerked back, like I had been poked. I'd had an abusive fiancé once, too. It was because of him that I'd ended up in Redemption.

Kat noticed my reaction and glanced up at me. "You, too?"

"It was a long time ago," I said evasively. "It's over now. But what about you? I'm so sorry to hear this happened to you."

She nodded slightly, her fingers starting to tear the newspaper into tiny shreds. "It's over for me, too. Abe is dead."

My mouth dropped open. "Dead?" Her story was starting to sound eerily close to mine, but I had no intention of going there. "What happened?"

Now, she began tearing the paper even faster. "It was a robbery gone bad. At least, that's what the cops have ruled it."

"Oh. How terrible. That must have been scary."

She nodded. "It was. I wasn't there, so I don't know what happened. But ..." she swallowed hard and looked away. "You see, the first time Ike and I saw each other, it was like meeting my soulmate. I knew he was the one. Just like he knew he was the one for me. But he was too honorable to do anything about it. Honestly, I would have." Her cheeks flushed again. "But he was clear that if I was engaged to another man, he wasn't interested. Of course, the problem was, I couldn't leave Abe. He ..." she paused to swallow hard. "He had made it clear if I tried to leave him, he would kill me."

I pressed a hand against my mouth. "Oh, Kat."

She nodded miserably. "I was trapped. I didn't know what to do."

"Did you tell Ike about the abuse?"

She looked away again. "Not right away. I was too ... embarrassed, I guess. Who gets involved with someone like that? I was a good person. I was brought up in a decent middle-class family. There was no good reason for getting myself so entangled with someone like Abe."

"People like Abe hide who they are," I said.

She quickly glanced toward me, her gaze sharp, before nodding. "You get it. Of course. When I first started dating Abe, he was wonderful. Treated me like a princess. I felt so lucky he had chosen me. But as time went on, he became more and more jealous and possessive. I couldn't go anywhere without his permission. He was becoming more critical of me, and I was starting to fear for my safety.

"Finally, one day I broke down and told Ike. He caught me in the middle of a weak moment. It had been a dreadful morning. Abe had ... well, it doesn't matter now. I was taking a moment in the teacher's lounge to gather myself for the day when Ike walked in and found me.

"He insisted I tell him what was going on. I couldn't do it right then, of course, as we had class. But he made me promise I would tell him after school. So, I did."

Kat paused for a long moment as she continued fiddling with the newspaper. "Anyway, he was shocked and horrified. Wanted me to leave Abe. I told him I couldn't … I was too afraid he would kill me. Ike said he understood and would help me get out.

"We became quite close during that time. He helped me gather my courage to leave Abe. So close, we …" she swallowed again, her mouth twisted up. "We were together the night Abe was killed."

"Oh. That's really rough," I said sympathetically. It was all starting to make more sense now.

She nodded, her face unhappy. "It was nothing we had planned," she insisted. "Ike, especially, was so careful. He was clear he didn't want to get involved until I had completely broken it off with Abe. And in my heart, I respected that. That's who I wanted to be with for the long haul—someone kind and caring and full of integrity.

"But I would be a liar if said I wasn't just a little bit … impatient." She gave me a small, secret smile. "So, when things started to heat up, I wasn't at all interested in stopping it. But when I got home and saw Abe sprawled out on the kitchen floor …" she squeezed her eyes shut and gave her head a quick shake, as if trying to knock the image out of her head. "Anyway, even though he was abusive—even though I wanted to leave him and be with Ike—something just … well, I guess something broke inside me. All the stress I had been living under for so long, day in and day out, along with the guilt and grief … and I just couldn't believe Abe was dead. Just like that. I had just seen him that morning, fully alive. How could he be gone? I couldn't sleep. I couldn't eat. I was completely overcome with emotion. It was … looking back, I think I was having a breakdown.

"Anyway, Ike was trying to help me through it, but I was … I was awful to him. You have to understand, I couldn't think straight. I wasn't myself. And one night …" she paused, biting her lips. "We had this horrible fight," she said, her words coming out in a rush. "I said some terrible things. Really … dreadful. I'm so ashamed of myself. The next day, I tried to call him to apologize, but he didn't pick up the phone. I decided to give him a few days to cool down. But then, I found out that he decided to quit his job and leave Sleepy Hollow. Just like that. He told one of my friends that he didn't think he could bear seeing me every day at school, so he decided he needed a clean slate." She was breathing hard, and I thought she might start crying, but after a moment, she composed herself.

"Anyway, I was beside myself. I knew I needed to find him, so I could properly apologize." She lifted her head and looked directly into my eyes, her gaze intense. "We're meant to be together. I know it, and he knows it. The fact that he left proves it. He knew it would be too painful for him to stay. Do you see why I'm so desperate to find him?"

"I do," I said. "I totally get it. So, you quit your job as well to look for him?"

She nodded. "What choice did I have? I was afraid if I didn't leave immediately, I would lose him forever. So, I've been trying to track him down. It wasn't easy, although thank goodness I at least knew he was working on the Midwestern edition. I had to guess at which towns he would visit and in what order, and I kept guessing wrong. I was completely spinning my wheels, having no idea where to look. I finally got so desperate, I hired a private investigator to help." Her expression was wry. "I guess I should have done that in the first place, huh?"

"What's important is you did it now," I said. "I'm glad it worked out."

A faint smile touched her lips. "Thank you. For everything. I had a feeling you would understand." She straightened in her chair. "Now, I guess all that's left is for me to wait here until Ike arrives."

"Hopefully, it won't be too long," I said, but I could tell she had stopped paying attention to me. Her gaze had shifted to one side, and her eyes narrowed.

"If you'll excuse me, I need to go," she said, her voice brusque. She started to push her chair back.

"Well, sure," I said, surprised and a bit taken aback. Was this a Sleepy Hollow thing? Did all the residents of that town customarily run out of a conversation so abruptly?

"Sorry, I have to deal with something … I'll be in touch." She shot me a tight smile and strode across the lobby.

I turned around, trying to see what had caused her reaction, but as far as I could tell, there was nothing there. An older couple sat on the couch looking at brochures, and a middle-aged man was relaxing in a chair near the fireplace reading the newspaper. A tall, thin man, his shoulders stooped, disappeared up the staircase, presumably going to his room. Kat seemed to ignore all of them, instead heading over to where Nancy stood behind the desk going through some paperwork, her silver reading glasses perched on her nose. As I watched, Nancy removed her glasses, and she and Kat exchanged a few words.

The skin at the back of my neck prickled, and I whirled around, certain I was being watched. I thought I saw a flash of something in the corner of my eye … a shadow of a person darting somewhere, but there was nothing there. Just the same people I had noticed before.

I kept watch for a moment, waiting to see if something appeared, but nothing did.

It must have been my imagination.

I turned back only to see Kat's back as she disappeared up the staircase, presumably finished with her conversion with Nancy, who had returned to the pile of work in front of her.

For a moment, I toyed with asking Nancy what Kat had said to her, but that felt like crossing a line. Kat WAS Nancy's customer, after all, and I didn't want to make Nancy feel uncomfortable talking about a paying guest. Not to mention it wasn't any of my business.

It was just so ... weird.

Was it possible both Kat and Ike had seen the same thing? Or was it just some sort of bizarre coincidence?

Or was there something else going on?

Chapter 8

The next morning, I woke in a foul mood. I hadn't slept well at all. I kept waking up, sure there was someone (or something) outside my house, but once I was awake, I heard nothing.

It didn't help that when I did fall asleep, my dreams were twisted and strange. Ike running from the bookstore, terror on his face, as he was chased by something dark and monstrous. Kat in the middle of the Redemption Inn's lobby, screaming and screaming. Wyle's expression was full of disappointment as he insisted it was all my fault.

All in all, it was a brutal night.

As soon as the sun peeked over the horizon, I was up and in the kitchen, brewing a pot of coffee. I wasn't a big coffee drinker, but if I was starting my day already grumpy and exhausted with a dull headache forming right behind my eyes, I was drinking coffee.

As I had some bananas that were starting to get a little over-ripe, I decided some banana bread may also hit the spot. While I was at it, a batch of banana-blueberry muffins sounded good, as well.

Of course, I couldn't eat all those baked goods myself. So, a call to Pat was in order, to invite her over for breakfast. She was more than happy to oblige.

I was in the middle of whipping up some more homemade dog biscuits—I had recently found that as small as Tiki was, she could eat twice her weight in dog biscuits with no issues—when I heard the door open.

"In the kitchen," I called out, spreading the batter in a small pan.

Tiki arrived first. I heard her little nails on the tile floor as she came trotting in and jumped up on my leg.

"I'll be with you in a moment," I told her as I finished scraping the bowl and popping the pan in the oven. I bent down to pet her, before realizing I hadn't heard Pat's voice.

"Pat?" I started straightening up only to see Pat standing in the corner of the kitchen, a peculiar look on her face. Alarm shot through me. "Is everything okay?"

"Have you started carving jack-o'-lanterns for Halloween yet?" Pat asked.

Ice-cold fingers seemed to trail down my spine. "No. Why do you ask?"

"Because there's one on your porch."

The ice then lodged in my chest, tightening my lungs and preventing me from breathing. I pushed past Pat and nearly ran to the front door, Pat and Tiki on my heels.

I threw open the front door and immediately saw it. There, on the porch step, a grinning jack-o'-lantern, his smile wide and jolly.

Except it wasn't really jolly. The more I looked at it, the more sinister the smile became, the cuts jagged and sharp across orange flesh, almost like teeth …

Pat joined me on the porch. "Man, that's creepy," she said.

I stepped toward it. "I have to get rid of it." The more I looked at it, the more it felt like I had manifested it. All the poking around I'd done over the past week into something that didn't concern me was now coming back to haunt me. *Maybe I should have stopped by the station after all last night*, I thought. *Maybe if I had told Wyle like I had promised him I would, this thing wouldn't be here.*

I wondered if I should toss it in the garbage or if it would be better to bury it in the garden, although it wouldn't surprise me if any plant that came in contact with it ended up rotting. I glanced down at my oversized long-sleeved tee shirt, wondering if I could somehow use it to pick up the atrocity, as I definitely didn't want to touch it.

Pat placed a gentle hand on my arm. "Let's call Wyle," she suggested. "I think he should see it first. And he probably wouldn't mind a cup of coffee and a fresh-baked muffin before heading into work."

As much as I wanted to get rid of the thing immediately, I knew Pat was right. It was time to call Wyle. Long past time. He needed to see this, just like he needed to know what happened yesterday.

I took a step back, brushing my hands off on my sweats, even though I hadn't gone near the carved pumpkin. "Okay. Let's give him a call."

***

"I'm confused," Wyle said, popping the last bite of his muffin into his mouth. "Did you say you heard something last night or not?" He had already eaten two, and Pat had eaten one plus a slice of banana bread. I hadn't been able to touch mine, although I had drunk one full cup of coffee loaded with cream and sugar, courtesy of Pat.

She had ended up taking charge, doctoring my coffee as I called Wyle, then telling me to sit down as she bustled around setting out the baked goods along with butter, plates, and napkins. She also made sure Tiki had a few treats.

"I'm not sure," I said. "I kept waking up, sure there was something outside, but I didn't hear anything."

"Then how did you know something was outside?"

"I don't know. Maybe I heard something while I was asleep that woke me?"

Wyle gave me a hard look. "But you're not aware of anything specific?"

I hunched over my coffee mug, cupping my hands around it. "No."

"Did you check outside?"

I shook my head.

He turned to Pat. "Did you see anything suspicious?"

"Other than an evil-looking jack-o'-lantern on the front porch? No."

"No strange cars or anything?"

Pat shook her head. Wyle jotted down a few notes and stood up. "Okay, I'm going to go have a look around. You two stay here. I'll be back in a minute."

"Ay ay, officer," I muttered. The coffee and sugar were doing their job, and even though I was still a little freaked out over the idea that someone was messing around in front of my house in the dead of night, I was feeling much more like myself.

Wyle shot me a look full of daggers before striding out of the kitchen.

Pat watched us, her eyes bright with interest. "Wyle seems a little … tense," she said, after we heard the door close, a slight smile playing on her lips. "Maybe he needs another muffin."

I sighed and rubbed my forehead. "What he thinks he needs is for me to stay out of the investigation," I said.

"Oooh," Pat breathed, breaking off a hunk of banana bread and shooting me a knowing look. "How long has he known you now? And he still hasn't figured out that's not an option?"

"I suspect it's a case of hope springs eternal." I sighed again and reached for a slice of banana bread. "I'm not looking forward to that conversation with him. Although in this case, it's my fault. I'm making a big deal out of nothing. It's probably just kids messing around."

"It sure seems like something kids would do," Pat agreed. "But regardless, it's happening more and more around here, and someone ought to get to the bottom of it, so it stops. If anyone can do that, it's Wyle."

I took a bite of the banana bread, trying to push down how uncomfortable I felt about not having shared my conversation with Ike yet. *As soon as Wyle comes back in, I will come clean*, I promised myself.

Pat was watching my face closely. "What's going on?" she asked, her voice suspicious.

I swallowed my bite and gave her an innocent look. "I'm drinking coffee and having some breakfast."

She made a face. "You know what I mean. Something else is going on. Spill it."

I sighed. "I was going to tell you, but then the jack-o'-lantern showed up and hijacked the conversation."

"No better time than the present."

"Yes, but Wyle should hear this, too."

Pat's eyes went wide. "Ohhh. So, *that's* what's going on." She nodded knowingly as she broke off more of her bread.

I narrowed my eyes. "What is THAT supposed to me?"

"Just that things make more sense now." She shot me a secret smile.

"Pat, what are you ..." I started to ask but paused as I heard the front door open and shut. A frowning Wyle appeared in the doorway. "Everything okay?" I asked.

"Other than the pumpkin, I don't see any evidence of anyone being here," he said.

"Oh. So, isn't that good news?" I asked.

His frown deepened. "It's not wise for a single woman like yourself to be living in such an isolated place alone."

"You're probably right, but since this is where my house is, I'm not sure how I can change that," I said.

"You could stop getting involved in cases," Wyle said. "That would help."

"Gail doesn't do any sleuthing, and she had jack-o'-lanterns show up on her porch," I pointed out. "She even heard a horse galloping by. I didn't hear that."

Wyle glowered at me. "You're increasing the odds that you'll become a target with your 'sleuthing,' as you call it."

"Not if we catch the bad guys quickly," I countered.

Wyle briefly closed his eyes. "Charlie, I swear ..."

"Okay, look," I interrupted. The longer I dragged it out, the worse it was going to be. "I know what you're going to say, but before you do, I just want to say you might be right."

There was a moment of shocked silence. Wyle's mouth dropped open in surprise as Pat set her mug on the table a little too hard, spilling coffee.

"Wait. Can you repeat that?" Wyle asked as he fumbled with his pockets. "I think I need to record this."

"Ha, ha," I said. "Just sit down and let me talk. I have a couple of things I need to tell you."

"Absolutely," he said, pulling his chair out to oblige. "I don't suppose there's any more coffee?"

"Are you kidding? There's always more coffee," Pat said, jumping to her feet. "I'll get it. I need to wipe up this spill anyway. And I bet you'd like another muffin as well, wouldn't you?"

"Don't mind if I do," Wyle said with a grin.

"You are in way too cheerful of a mood," I grumbled.

"Well, it's not every day you admit I'm right," he said, leaning back and crossing his arms. "So, let's hear it."

I eyed Pat, who was bringing the coffee pot over to refill the mugs. I wondered if I should wait for her to be done, but I decided I needed to quit stalling. "I saw Ike yesterday," I said.

Wyle's expression didn't change. "And?"

"And, according to him, this isn't the first time this has happened."

Wyle stared at me, his face starting to arrange itself into what I thought of as his "cop face."

"And, by 'this,' you mean …"

"The jack-o'-lanterns and sound of a horse galloping," I said.

"Seriously?" Pat exclaimed, taking her attention off of refilling my mug and pouring coffee all over the table. "Oh, for Pete's sake," she said, mopping it up with the washcloth in her other hand. "I better make another pot."

"You better start from the beginning," Wyle directed, uncrossing his arms and digging his notebook and pen out of his pocket.

I quickly filled both of them in on how I ran into Ike at the Quote the Raven bookstore, the strange conversation we had, and the abrupt way he ran off.

"Did he tell you the names of the other towns?" Wyle asked as he frantically scribbled in his notebook.

"No."

Wyle muttered something under his breath. "I don't suppose you asked him to come see me."

"That didn't come up, either," I said. Wyle shot me a look. "Honest. I had every intention of telling him he needed to go see you, but he ran out before I could."

Wyle grunted and reached for his coffee. "That does seem to be a theme with him."

"Maybe he really is being haunted," Pat said. She was back in her regular seat, having successfully refilled our coffees, cleaned up the table, and set out more muffins and banana bread. Tiki was on her lap and happily nosing around for crumbs.

"You think the Headless Horseman is following him around from town to town?" Wyle asked skeptically.

"Well, it would certainly explain how jumpy he is," Pat answered before raising her eyebrow at Wyle. "I bet you would be pretty jumpy, too, if the Headless Horseman was following you."

"I would definitely be jumpy if that was happening to me," Wyle said. "But I'm not convinced that's what's going on."

"Who else could it be?" Pat argued. "It can't very well be a bunch of kids coordinating in all these different towns."

"First of all, we haven't established that any of this even happened anywhere other than here," Wyle said. "But if it turns out to be true, the most obvious reason would be that Ike's behind it."

"Or his publisher," I said. "It's true this seems more like a publicity stunt than anything else. But …"

Wyle looked like he was trying not to roll his eyes. "But what?" he asked, reaching over to grab a muffin.

"But he just didn't seem like he was acting," I said. "He seemed sincerely afraid."

"If you're a good enough actor, it won't seem like you're acting," Wyle said.

"I know," I said. "And what you're saying makes sense. But that's not the only strange thing that happened yesterday."

"Don't you dare tell me you saw the Headless Horseman," Wyle said with a groan.

"No, nothing like that. I told you, I didn't hear or see anything until that jack-o'-lantern showed up on my porch." I shivered despite myself and clutched my mug tighter. "But I did meet Ike's ex-girlfriend."

"You what?" Pat yelped, spilling her coffee a third time. Tiki yipped in surprise, too. "Oh, for goodness' sake. That's it for coffee for me today."

Wyle also looked surprised. "Ike's ex-girlfriend is in Redemption?"

"Apparently," I said.

"Does Ike know?" Pat asked.

"It didn't seem like it, at least as of yesterday when I spoke to her," I said.

"Of course you would be the one to run into the ex-girlfriend," Wyle muttered before fixing me with a hard look. "How did you possibly end up meeting her?"

I filled them in about going to the Redemption Inn to try and give Ike the book he wanted and instead running into Kat.

Wyle was back to his frantic note taking. "So, you're saying Kat's fiancé was murdered?"

"That's what she said."

"In Sleepy Hollow?"

"Apparently."

"What a twisted love triangle," Pat said.

"You can say that again," Wyle agreed. "I'll call over there and see what I can dig up about that case."

There was something about Wyle's expression and tone that gave me pause. "Wait. You don't think Ike had anything to do with Abe's death, do you?"

"I don't know what to think," Wyle said grimly. "Except I find it very suspicious that a few months ago, Ike was involved with a woman whose fiancé was murdered, and now, he appears to be involved in some very odd pranks in various towns."

"He's claiming he's not involved, though," I said. "It's the Headless Horseman doing it."

"Maybe the Headless Horseman killed Abe, too," Pat threw out.

"The fact that all these things are happening around Ike and he's claiming not to have anything to do with them is also suspicious," Wyle said.

Wyle had a point, and I didn't think he was completely wrong. There did seem to be some sort of connection between Kat, Ike, and the pranks. Especially when you considered that the pranks only happened to people who owned haunted houses and Ike was not only a ghost hunter, but also researching haunting houses.

But what would be the connecting thread? Other than Ike himself being the one behind it all?

"Do you think it's all connected?" Pat asked Wyle.

"I don't know, but I intend to find out," he said before eyeing me. "Anything else you want to share?"

"Not at the moment."

He frowned as he picked up his coffee. "You know what I'm going to say."

"To let the professionals investigate," I said.

He put his cup down without drinking from it. "Charlie, this is serious," he said. "You were just targeted. You do understand you could be playing with fire."

"I know," I said. "But again, I'm not the only one who has gotten one of those hideous jack-o'-lanterns. And as you pointed out, it was actually stranger when I wasn't experiencing any of these things, considering I am living in the most haunted house in Redemption."

Wyle stared intently at me, the expression in his eyes unreadable. "Charlie, this isn't a game. Your actions could be making you a target."

"I'll be careful," I said, keeping my voice light while trying not to reveal how much his words unnerved me. Even though I had half-expected to eventually see a jack-o'-lantern on my porch, actually finding it creeped me out more than I wanted to admit. Knowing someone was sneaking around my yard while I was sleeping inside was troubling. Even though I told myself I wasn't being targeted any more than any other haunted-house owner, I couldn't completely push away the uneasy feeling that I had attracted more attention to myself than I had bargained for.

Wyle opened his mouth—presumably to argue with me—when Pat suddenly cried out, "Tiki, no!"

Tiki was standing on her hind legs nosing Midnight, who was curled up in his usual chair next to the window. Both Pat and I jumped to our feet. I was sure Midnight was going to tear the little dog apart, probably with one swipe from his impressive claws. He was not a cat you wanted to mess with. Nearly twenty pounds of pure muscle, little Tiki wouldn't stand a chance.

Instead, much to my surprise, Midnight simply picked up his head and nosed Tiki back.

"My word," Pat said as we glanced at each other. "Do you think they'll end up friends after all?"

"We can only hope," I said.

"I need to go," Wyle announced, standing up as well as he drained the last of his coffee. He shot me a hard look. "Charlie, be careful."

"Promise," I said.

He didn't look convinced as he headed out the door.

I looked back to Midnight. He had stopped nosing Tiki and put his head down, a self-satisfied smug look on his feline face.

If I didn't know better, I would have sworn he distracted Wyle on purpose.

Chapter 9

"Is this Charlie Kingsley?"

I adjusted the receiver between my shoulder and ear. I didn't recognize the voice. It was muffled, as if whoever was on the other end was calling from a payphone. "This is she."

"I'm calling on behalf of Ike Krane. Would you be able to meet him in an hour at The Tipsy Cow?"

"Who is this?"

"A friend. Can you meet him?"

I knew I should say no. Wyle's warnings were still ping-ponging around my head, and I couldn't completely convince myself that I hadn't inadvertently brought this on myself. Not to mention that jack-o'-lantern, which also continued to bother me. Wyle had taken it with him, and I was glad I didn't have to look at it anymore. Still, the image was burned into my brain.

The smart play would be to decline. Except I really wanted to know why Ike had run out on me a second time. And why was someone else reaching out to me instead of Ike? Was there something else going on? Was Ike in hiding? Of course, he wouldn't want to meet me at The Tipsy Cow if that were the case.

And how did Kat and her dead fiancé fit into all of this?

I really, really had no business getting involved. For once, I knew I should listen to Wyle and let him do his job to get to the bottom of whatever was going on.

On the other hand, it was also possible that the fastest way to stop it all was for me to get to figure out precisely what was going on with Ike. And maybe Kat, too.

"Okay," I said.

"See you then," the caller said. At least, that was what I thought the caller said. The words came out in a rush before he or she hung up.

I replaced the receiver and glanced at the clock. I had been getting ready to start dinner, but the roast chicken I planned was no longer going to work. There was just enough time for me to prepare and eat a quick meal of pasta with leftover meat sauce and a salad. Once I finished, I took a few moments to freshen up—changing into a sweater, adding some jewelry, and running a comb through my hair. *He has a girlfriend*, I reminded myself as I added a little lip gloss. *And, even if he didn't, I'm not interested.* Things were complicated enough with Wyle. I didn't need to add Ike into the mix.

But if looking nice might help me get a little more information, I wasn't above the extra effort.

I wondered if I should call Wyle and let him know I was about to meet Ike, but almost immediately decided against it. Ike seemed to be skittish enough without a cop making things worse, and the last thing I wanted to do was give him an excuse to run out yet again. I definitely wanted some answers, and this might be my best shot at getting them. Knowing Wyle wanted answers, as well, I sent him a silent promise that I would do my best to convince Ike to go see him.

Right when I was about to leave, the phone rang again, and my heart sank. Was this Ike canceling? Or more accurately, the mysterious assistant? But when I answered, there was no one there. *Probably a wrong number*, I thought as I replaced the receiver and headed out the door.

I arrived at The Tipsy Cow five minutes early. I didn't see Ike anywhere, so I went to the bar to order a glass of white wine. The place was half-empty, but I wasn't that surprised, as it was a weekday night and a little too late for the after-work crowd.

The bartender had just placed the wine in front of me when I heard a slightly nasal voice from behind me. "Charlie, right?"

I turned around. A tall, thin man with stooped shoulders and thinning hair stood behind me. He seemed familiar, but I couldn't place it.

"Yes, I'm Charlie."

He smiled, but it didn't reach his eyes. "I'm David. I'm the one who called you."

I turned around on the bar stool. "Nice to meet you, David." I craned my neck, trying to see further into the bar. "Is Ike here? I don't see him."

"Can we talk for a minute?" he asked, gesturing toward a row of empty booths off to the side. I nodded as I slid off the barstool and collected my wine. He led me to a booth that had a half-empty beer, notebook, and pen on the table. He gestured to the empty side.

"So, how do you know Ike?" I asked as he slid into the seat across from me.

He smiled again, but this one seemed a little more embarrassed. "I'm afraid I have a confession."

"Oh?" My eyes quickly darted around The Tipsy Cow, trying to gauge whether there was anyone close by who could help if this little meeting started to go south. Unfortunately, the booth was near the back, and we were alone.

"I'm a reporter," he said.

My eyes shifted back to him, and I blinked in surprise. "A reporter?"

He nodded. "I'm investigating Ike."

"Why?"

His gaze was steady. "For killing Abe Hammish."

"Abe Hammish? Are you talking about Kat's fiancé?"

"That's the one."

I looked at him in confusion. "But I thought Abe was killed during a botched robbery."

His lips twisted into a sardonic smile. "That is what Ike would like you to think."

I almost corrected him, seeing how it wasn't Ike who had told me that, but Kat. But then I decided it might be more prudent to hold back that tidbit of information. "What about the cops? Are you saying they also suspect Ike?"

David's mouth flattened into a thin line. "No, they believe the robbery-gone-bad lie, as well. Unfortunately, Ike was able to convince them of his innocence, too."

"But presumably, they investigated," I persisted. The image of Ike with a teasing grin and warm expression in his deep brown eyes behind his horn-rimmed glasses flashed in my mind. The idea of him being the one who killed Abe seemed preposterous.

David pressed his lips together even tighter. "They claim they did."

"But you don't believe it."

He shrugged. "Mistakes happen. That's the charitable view."

"And the uncharitable one?"

He flashed his sardonic smile again. "Cops bury the truth all the time, whether because of corruption, blackmail, a mistake they don't want to admit, or to protect someone. The list goes on and on."

"Wow." I picked up my wine. Not because I wanted to drink it, but more to hold something in my hands. I wasn't sure how I felt being tucked away in a back booth with a man who thought Ike was not just a murderer, but cold-blooded enough to get the police department to dismiss the case. Had I been that wrong about him? Was he really that bad? Or was David delusional? "You really don't like Ike, do you?"

"Ike is dangerous," David said flatly. "If you know what's good for you, you'll stay far away."

I stared at David. Dangerous? I pictured Ike again, this time all gangly legs and elbows. Unless you were a piece of paper and there was a beer nearby, I didn't see him as all that dangerous. "Do you have any actual proof of that?"

"He killed my aunt."

I was so shocked, I nearly dropped my glass of wine into my lap. Instead, I ended up only spilling it. Luckily, it was white.

"Oh, shoot," I said, grabbing the napkin my wine had been sitting on to dab at my sweater. Without a word, David handed me his napkin, as well.

"Thanks," I said as I continued to mop at the wet spot. I waited another moment to see if he would continue to talk, but when he remained silent, I decided I would have to prod him. "How did Ike kill your aunt?"

David looked away and didn't immediately answer. I was still cleaning myself up, so I stayed quiet as well. "My aunt and uncle had an amazing love affair," he said. "They were childhood sweethearts and married for nearly 40 years. They were true soulmates and an inspiration to everyone who saw them together. They were the couple who always held hands and laughed at inside jokes.

"So, when he got cancer and died, you can imagine how devastated my aunt was. She was completely unable to function. My mother, that's her sister, did everything she could. But my aunt was despondent without my uncle. She didn't want to live without him.

"That's where Ike entered the story."

He paused again, a sour expression on his face, like he had just eaten a lemon. After a sip of beer, he continued. "You should understand that my aunt never worked outside the home. My uncle had made a very good living, and even though they didn't have children, my aunt's life revolved around taking care of him. He had set her up financially, so she wouldn't have to worry. But she couldn't handle not having him there to take care of. At first, she was so depressed, she wouldn't get out of bed. It didn't matter what anyone said to her—she didn't want to live without my uncle. Until the day she got the idea to try and contact his spirit."

I closed my eyes. Suddenly, I could see where David's story was going.

"So, she started going to all these mediums and seances. It was …" he shook his head. "Again, my mother—along with the rest of the family—was beside herself. She was convinced some scam artist was going to take all my aunt's money, and then what would she do? She had no skills, no jobs other than a couple of summer gigs back when she was in school. But there was no talking to my aunt, let alone dissuading her. She was determined to communicate with my uncle beyond the grave.

"Eventually, she got the bright idea that my uncle's spirit was haunting her house. I'm not sure where it came from—probably one of the mediums wanting to scam her into some sort of retainer relationship. But she was convinced he had never left … that he was still watching over her. She was ecstatic and, of course, she wanted to communicate with him in the house, which is how Ike got involved.

"I have no idea how she met him or found out about him or anything. All I know is that she was so excited she had found him, because he was going to 'prove' that my uncle was still with her in her home, taking care of her beyond the grave."

David paused again to drink more beer, his expression dark. "Ike took advantage of her. He ended up swindling her out of a large sum of money before deserting her, and she ended up dying of a broken heart."

"My goodness," I said. I was shocked at what I had just heard. I didn't take Ike as a con artist, and honestly thought it a bit of a stretch to call him a "murderer" in that scenario. "What a dreadful tragedy. I'm so sorry for your loss."

David inclined his head. "Thank you. It was over ten years ago. My mother still hasn't gotten over it. She misses her sister terribly."

"I can imagine. What a horrible way to lose a sibling."

We were quiet for a moment. David drained his beer while I reached for my wine glass but didn't drink. "I'm curious, though. And I'm not trying to be insensitive, but did anyone call the cops over Ike stealing your aunt's money?"

David let out a loud sigh. "No. And not for lack of trying. My mom wanted her to file a report, but my aunt was too distraught to do anything but lie in bed. It was like my uncle had died all over again. She couldn't get up, couldn't do anything. Until she just … died."

"Wow, that's just … I'm so sorry," I said again. "Did anyone try to confront Ike or ask him about it?"

David snorted. He hadn't let go of his empty mug yet, and I could see fingers tighten around the glass. "Are you kidding? You think that weasel would admit to any wrongdoing?"

I took that to mean David had personally tried to talk to Ike, which then brought up more questions in my head. "Where did this all take place? Was it in Sleepy Hollow or some other town?"

"It was in Sleepy Hollow," David said, his expression brooding. I noticed his fingers were nearly white, he was clutching the beer mug so hard, and I started to get a little nervous he might crack it. "My whole family is from there. I've known Ike since grade school. He was always a weasel. And as my mom always said, 'A weasel never changes its spots. They only get bigger.'"

Somehow, I didn't think that was the saying, but I also didn't think it was the time or place to correct him.

"But what he did to my aunt was next level," David continued. "I'll never forgive him for that."

"I can imagine," I said. "It was a terrible thing for your family to go through. I can understand why you might think Ike had something to do with Abe's murder. But is there also some evidence that he was involved? Something that maybe the police overlooked?"

David's expression was bemused. "That was much nicer than what others have said about my theory. Look, I get it. I sound a bit … intense."

"Well …" I said with a helpless smile. "Intense" was one word for it, although not the only one I would have chosen.

He leaned toward me. "If I told you Ike was there that night, would that change things for you?"

My jaw dropped. "Seriously?"

He nodded solemnly. "One of the neighbors saw him walking down the street. It was late … definitely after Abe had been killed."

"That … well, that does change things," I said. "Do the police know?"

David sat back, his face disgusted. "Of course. I told you, they're corrupt."

"I don't understand. Why wouldn't they go after him?"

"You'd have to ask them," David said, his face twisted in loathing.

I looked at him in confusion. "They didn't give you an explanation?"

David shook his head in exasperation. "Look, it doesn't matter what they said. The point is, we need to put pressure on them to do the right thing and charge Ike, so he stops hurting innocent people."

"And by 'pressure,' do you mean public pressure?" I asked. "Like what would happen if you published an article?"

"Exactly," David said. He flattened his hands against the table and leaned closer to me, his eyes full of passion and righteousness. "That's why I'm here. I want to expose Ike once and for all. It's time someone held him accountable for his actions."

"Okay," I said, leaning back as far as I could in the narrow booth. His intensity was starting to scare me a bit. "So, why did you call me?"

He looked at me like I was an idiot. "Because I need your help."

"How can I possibly help you?"

"Because Ike knows who I am, but he wouldn't suspect you."

I stared at him in bewilderment. This journalist, who may not even be a journalist, now that I thought about it, considering he hadn't shown me credentials or even a published article with his byline, was expecting me to join forces with him? "Are you asking me to ... spy on Ike for you?"

"Well, yeah." His expression seemed to suggest he was seriously reconsidering asking me, as I might be too dumb to help him after all. "How else am I going to get what I need for my story?"

"That's a good question. And I can appreciate why you need help, but I'm less clear as to why I should get involved."

He titled his head. "Don't you want to know the truth about Ike?" He seemed genuinely baffled by my response.

"Well, yeah, but I'm hardly in a position to get it," I said. "You do understand I just met him, right?"

He frowned. "But you were looking for him at the Redemption Inn. So there must be some sort of connection."

All my senses went on high alert. "How did you know I was looking for him at the inn?" It also suddenly occurred to me that David had never answered my question about how he found me.

"Because I saw you there," he said. "I walked right by you. Didn't you see me?"

The image of the stooped man disappearing up the steps flashed in my head. "Actually, I do remember seeing you now," I said. "But why did you think I was there for Ike?"

He again had that disappointed expression on his face, presumably assuming I was turning out to be an exceptionally dim-witted partner in justice. "Because I overheard what you said to the owner. You were asking if Ike was staying there. I thought you said you saw me."

"I did, but it was … later." My eyes narrowed in suspicion. "Have you been stalking me?"

His mouth dropped open. "No! It isn't like that. I was in that breakfast room doing some work when I overheard you ask the owner about Ike, so I came out to see who it was. But before I could say anything, I saw Kat approach you."

The pieces were starting to slide into place. "You know Kat?"

"Of course I know Kat. She's part of the story."

"Have you gotten Kat's version of what happened to Abe?"

David's face went still. "She's saying what she has to say."

My jaw went slack. This conversation was getting more and more peculiar. "What is THAT supposed to mean?"

"Just what it sounds like." His expression was shut down, and I could tell the conversation was closed. "It's not important anyway. So, will you help?"

I held my palms up in the air in exasperation. "Help? Help with what? I still don't understand what you're asking me to do."

"Ask Ike what happened the night Abe died," David said.

"And what will that accomplish?"

"We need to get him to contradict himself," David answered. "Then I'll be able to run with the discrepancy."

"But I don't know what he originally said, so how am I going to know if he contradicts himself?" I asked.

"You don't have to," David said as he started fumbling in his bag. "I'll know."

This so-called plan was sounding more ridiculous by the minute. "So, you're expecting me to remember what Ike says word for word? Or should I be taking notes while he's talking?"

"Neither," David said triumphantly as he located whatever he was digging around for in his bag. With a flourish, he placed it in the center of the table.

I stared at it, momentarily speechless.

"Is that ... what I think it is?" I asked.

"Trust me, it's state of the art," David said. "You'll be amazed what it picks up."

I looked back down at the object, which appeared to be a very ordinary-looking hand-held tape recorder. "You expect me to *record* my conversation with Ike?"

"Well, yes. How else am I going to prove he's not telling the truth?"

I briefly closed my eyes. "David, this is an insane plan. First off, I don't even know where Ike is ..."

"You know he's staying at the Redemption Inn," David interrupted. "You can leave a message with the owner to have him call you. He will. And I'm staying there, too, so I can also keep an eye out for him."

Apparently, everyone was staying at the Redemption Inn. At least Nancy was making a few bucks out of this mess. "Okay, but what you don't seem to understand is that I don't know Ike very well. How do you expect me to bring up Abe in the first place?"

"You met Kat," David pointed out. "I'm sure you can figure out some way to work it into the conversation." His expression seemed less sure than his words. I wondered if he was still thinking about how I wasn't catching on fast enough to his grand plan.

"You're still assuming he's going to tell me the truth," I said. "Or at least something different than he told the cops."

"As you pointed out, he only just met you, so he has no reason to lie to you," David said. "Plus, you're not from Sleepy Hollow. You don't know any of the players or what really happened. Why bother to lie?"

"He also has no reason to tell me the truth."

"Well, we at least need to try," David said stubbornly, pushing the small recorder toward me. "I know Ike is pretty smart, but he has to mess up sometime. Once you have his story on tape, I can go over it until I find some sort of discrepancy."

I stared at the tape recorder, but I didn't touch it. "David, I'm not doing this."

He blinked at me. "What do you mean? Why not?"

"Because it's nuts."

"What's nuts?"

I gestured with my hand. "This whole plan. It's crazy. I'm not going to start interrogating someone I've barely met about an event I have no knowledge of."

David's mouth opened and shut like a fish struggling for air. "But you have to," he said. "How else am I going to prove his guilt?"

"I guess you'll need to find someone else willing to secretly record Ike," I said as I collected my things. "Or think of a new plan."

"Wait, don't go," David pleaded as he went back to rummaging in his bag. "Here." He thrust a card at me. "My pager number is on there. I have it with me at all times."

"Why would I page you?"

"Well, when you're talking to Ike," David said. "Page me and tell me where you are, and I'll worry about the recording."

This was even more absurd than the last plan. "So, let me get this straight. The next time I see Ike, you want me to excuse myself, page you, wait there for you to call me back so I can tell you where I'm at, then go back to Ike and make small talk with him until you show up and somehow get close enough to record him without him seeing you, at which point, I start asking him questions about Abe?"

He looked uncomfortable. "It would be easier if you took the recorder. Or maybe you can arrange a time and place to meet Ike, and then let me know where you're going, so I can worry about the logistics."

"It doesn't matter who has the recorder. It's not going to be easy," I said.

"Nothing worthwhile is easy," he responded matter-of-factly. "That doesn't mean it isn't worth doing."

"I suppose," I said, although I wasn't sure how much I agreed with him about any of this being all that worthwhile. It seemed more like grasping at straws.

I still hadn't taken the card, and he shoved it a little closer to me. I glanced at it but didn't touch it. It was a simple, white card with only his name, phone number, and pager number. Under his name, it read "Independent Investigative Journalist."

I glanced up at David. "Independent?"

He sat up straighter. "Yes. I'm beholden to no one, which means I can focus solely on finding the truth."

I almost asked him if that also meant he wasn't employed, but I decided it wasn't fair. Back when I lived in New York, I had known a couple freelance writers, one of whom was a budding novelist by night and wrote for a magazine during the day. If you landed the right gigs, it could be lucrative, especially if you were also savvy about reselling your articles to other magazines.

So, it wasn't that I had any issue with him working for himself. It was just how pompous he was being about it. Actually, now that I thought about it, maybe the right word was "defensive." I wondered if it was a sore spot, because he had gotten himself fired at some point. If that were the case, I really didn't need to be rubbing it in.

Either way, it wasn't my business. It had nothing to do with me. It wasn't like I had any intention of getting involved with his scheme. I was about to refuse to even take his card when I reconsidered and picked it up. Maybe Wyle would want to get in touch with him about the whole Abe situation.

"You can page me day or night. I don't care," David said, the words coming out in a rush, as if he were afraid I would change my mind.

I decided I didn't want to know why he thought I would be meeting up with Ike in the middle of the night. I simply nodded and dropped the card in my bag. "I need to go," I said, sliding out of the booth.

"You'll page me the next time you see Ike?" David asked as I stood up. Desperation tinged his voice.

"I'll do what I can," I said. I was hoping that was lukewarm enough to not give him any false hope, but David's reaction was to give me a huge, relieved smile.

"Thank you! I knew I could count on you," he said.

I held up my hand. "I said I would do what I can. No promises."

"Of course. I know. Thank you. You don't know what this means."

"I get it," I said, taking a step back. "I have to go."

David continued talking, but I stopped listening. Something had caught my eye, and I turned to face the main bar.

The bar had gotten busier during my conversation with David, which made sense, as it was later in the evening. As I scanned the room, I wasn't sure what had gotten my attention.

But then I saw her, and I could feel my heart sink in my chest. I wasn't even sure why, as it wasn't like I was doing anything wrong by meeting David.

My nemesis, Louise, was watching me from one of the booths, a small smirk on her lips.

Chapter 10

I bolted straight up in bed. Was that what I thought it was?

My bedroom was pitch-black other than the numbers on my clock radio next to my bed. 3:00 am. The witching hour.

The window shade was up, as I liked waking up to the sun rising, but it was as dark outside as it was in my room. There was no moon, and the night was empty and still.

Or was it?

I was sure I had heard something outside.

"You heard it, too, didn't you?" I whispered to Midnight. He was lying on the pillow next to me, but his head was raised, and I could see his eyes glancing around. He normally didn't let much disturb him, and usually, when something woke me in the middle of the night, he was more interested in watching me than anything else. But even he seemed more watchful and alert.

"You DID hear it, didn't you?" I asked. "I know what I heard. I'm sure of it. It sounded like ... "

Clop, clop, clop.

There it was—the sound of a horse galloping on the road, accompanied by a loud neigh.

For a moment, I couldn't move. I could only sit there, frozen and petrified in my bed, listening intently to the sound of hooves striking the asphalt and the loud, screaming neighing.

It couldn't really be the Headless Horseman. Could it?

No. It was a prank. Kids. That's all.

Still, I couldn't bring myself to move. As much as my logical mind was sure it was nothing more than child's play, part of me was terrified it truly was the Headless Horseman, somehow brought to life by a hapless Ike. And now, he was following him from town to town, looking for people to steal away, so they would never be seen again ...

Stop that. I gave myself a quick shake. *Enough.* I had to get myself under control. If I didn't, and failed to get to the bottom of what was behind all this haunting, it was never going to stop.

That was the thought that got me out of bed. I wasn't going to allow whatever it was to disturb my sleep or chase me out of my home.

I ran to the window, peering out into the darkness. Of course, I couldn't see anything. Not only was it too dark, but my bedroom faced my backyard, and the sound of the hooves was definitely a result of striking asphalt.

I flew across the bedroom, flung open the door, and ran down the hallway. My living room window would be the best place to see the street, and I hurried to get down to it as fast as I could, the sound of the horse hooves growing louder as I got closer to the front of the house.

I had just made it to the window and pulled back the curtain when it stopped.

As quickly and abruptly as it had started.

I leaned closer to the window, straining my eyes to see if I could make anything out in the darkness. My breathing was harsh in my ears, especially noticeable now that there were no sounds cutting through the silence.

But it was too dark to make out much of anything.

I snapped on the front porch light, blinking as the sudden brightness blinded me. Hopefully, it startled whoever was outside as well, and I could catch a glimpse of them in the light.

Unfortunately, my porch light wasn't bright enough to illuminate much more than my front yard and driveway. I still couldn't make out much of the street, either, and from what I could see, there wasn't anything there.

The minutes ticked by as I stood watching, my nose nearly pressed against the glass, frantically searching the yard for a sign. But there was nothing.

Finally, in frustration, I backed away from the window. If it was kids, they were long gone, and it seemed there would be no repeat performance, at least for the time being. And that meant my chance of catching them was also gone.

I reached out my hand to turn the porch light off, but at the last moment, I decided to leave it on. If, for some reason, whoever was responsible did decide to come back for an encore, I'd have a better chance of catching them.

I also hesitated by my front door. I didn't have a clear view of my porch, so I couldn't see if there was a jack-o'-lantern there or not. Part of me felt like I ought to check, but another figured it would be perfectly acceptable to wait until morning.

After all, I reasoned as I headed toward the staircase, what would I do if I found one there? Call Wyle and wake him up in the middle of the night? Call the station and talk to one of the few all-night-duty officers who likely had more urgent things to deal with than a pumpkin left on a porch? Morning seemed soon enough to deal with it.

I was just stepping up on the bottom stair when I rethought my plan to go back to bed. While I was definitely still tired, I was also wired and fairly certain I wouldn't be able to fall asleep any time soon.

With a sigh, I turned and went into the kitchen to make a pot of tea. I'd wait a few hours before brewing a pot of coffee. I was also considering making homemade cinnamon rolls. After all, everything was better with a homemade cinnamon roll. And after my evening with David and having my sleep interrupted by whatever that was, I needed a good pick-me-up.

Midnight joined me as I was finishing the tea, clearly expecting an early breakfast. I fed him and sat at the kitchen table where I could watch the sun come up. Once I drank a cup of my breakfast blend, I'd start the cinnamon rolls.

I rubbed my forehead, already feeling a headache forming behind my eyes. Actually, it had started the night before, after seeing Louise.

There had been a time when Louise and I were friends. When I moved to Redemption, she was one of the first people I'd met, and she helped make me not only feel welcomed, but a part of a community.

I had never really felt that before. Growing up in New York, I always felt like an outsider … a square peg in a round hole. My family never understood me, and my friends had all been the fair-weather type—always up for a party, but the moment the alcohol ran out, they had somewhere else to be.

I still felt grateful to Louise for making me feel so at home when I first arrived, terrified and alone. She never asked questions or passed judgment … just accepted me for who I was.

Until her brother Jesse and his best friend disappeared.

She blamed me for it, despite there being no proof of my being involved. She was convinced it was my fault, even though Pat and others had tried to persuade her otherwise. I personally thought she needed someone to blame. She had a terrible fight with Jesse before he disappeared, and I had a feeling the guilt was almost too much for her to bear. I was an easy scapegoat, as unlike everyone else in Redemption, I hadn't been raised here. In that sense, I was an outsider.

Unfortunately, she had then made it her mission to drive me out of Redemption, and every chance she got, she tried to turn as many people as she could against me, hoping that would convince me to leave. Unfortunately for her, I had no intention of going anywhere. Ever. Redemption was my home, and here I would stay.

But that didn't mean she couldn't make my life difficult.

My mind kept picturing her self-satisfied smirk as she watched me with David. For the life of me, I couldn't figure out what she was thinking. So what that I had a drink with David? I wasn't dating anyone, and even if I was in a relationship, it still wouldn't have mattered, because nothing had happened between David and me.

I suspected she was just messing with my head. Still, it bothered me. I couldn't stop thinking she might know something about David that I didn't.

I also couldn't stop wondering if whatever it was might end up coming back to haunt me.

Chapter 11

Wyle immediately spotted me the moment I walked into the police-station lobby. His brow furrowed as he strode toward me, and I could feel my stomach slowly sink as I studied the expression on his face.

I had taken time with my appearance that morning. The nights of broken sleep were catching up with me, and I didn't want Wyle using the circles under my eyes as an excuse to badger me into staying out of the investigation. But judging by Wyle's expression, I hadn't been all that successful.

"What happened?" Wyle asked.

"Good morning to you, too," I said.

Wyle eyed me. "That's still to be determined, although the fact you're here doesn't bode well for it being a good morning."

"That's not very nice," I said. "Didn't your mother teach you any manners?"

He folded his arms across his broad chest. "Out with it, Charlie. What happened?"

"I baked cinnamon rolls this morning," I said, holding out the Tupperware container. "And you definitely look like someone who could use a homemade, freshly baked cinnamon roll."

Wyle glared at me, but I could see his resolve weakening. He took the container. "Come on, let's go back to my desk."

I followed him through the lobby, weaving my way around the other officers' desks. As it was still early, most of them were standing around drinking coffee and chatting. "Hey, Wyle," one of them called out. "What's that you got?" He nodded toward the Tupperware.

"None of your beeswax," Wyle said, and the officer laughed.

Wyle gestured for me to have a seat while he went for coffee. "I assume you don't want a cup," he said.

I shook my head. "I had more than my share at home." Which was true, but there was also no way I was going to drink that sludge they referred to as "coffee."

I perched on the hard plastic chair, wondering if I had made a mistake showing up at the station instead of just calling him and having him come out to the house. At the time, I thought telling Wyle about David in a more neutral environment would be best. I knew he or another officer would eventually come out to the house to look around, but I didn't think there was any urgency to it. I had already walked the neighborhood that morning as soon as there was enough light, and I hadn't seen anything out of the ordinary, although I wasn't sure what I thought I'd find. We hadn't gotten a lot of rain, so the ground was dry and mostly covered with a colorful array of dead leaves.

In fact, breathing in the crisp fall air that smelled of decaying leaves as the cheery sun rose in the sky, I even wondered if I had just imagined the whole thing. It seemed impossible to reconcile the eerie sound of a horse galloping in the dead of night on such a lovely autumn morning.

But no, I knew I hadn't. Something had been out there last night. I just wished I had some clue as to what that something was.

Was it Ike? It was true that everything seemed to start upon his arrival, which pointed to him being behind it in some way, whether personally or by association with someone connected to him, like his publisher or a public relations agency. But despite the publicity-stunt explanation making the most sense, something about it didn't seem right.

What about David? He certainly seemed to hate Ike enough to pin something on him. He also seemed like the kind of guy who would love to torture Ike by making him think he was being haunted by the Headless Horseman. But that seemed to be an awful lot of work and effort, especially considering David seemed more consumed with getting Ike arrested for Abe's murder. Why would he waste his time and energy with ridiculous pranks?

And speaking of Abe's murder, how did Kat fit into all of it? And what did David mean when he said Kat was "doing what she had to do"? Was it because she was experiencing some sort of trauma? I knew firsthand how much trauma an abused partner continuously endured, especially when you couple it with the shock of a murder. It didn't surprise me that Kat had experienced a breakdown. Was that what David had been referring to … that Kat was in a fragile state?

The whole story was just bizarre. And while it could just be a coincidence that some kids decided to pull a Headless-Horseman-based prank just as someone named Ike Krane from Sleepy Hollow was visiting, I couldn't buy it.

They were connected somehow. I knew it.

I also knew the next step was to tell Wyle what was going on, even though I was dreading his reaction. And that's why I decided the best thing to do was to go to the station and tell him there … although the knowing looks the officers kept casting in my direction made me think I had made the wrong decision.

Wyle returned with his coffee and sat down behind his desk, smoothing his shirt. He balanced the Tupperware container on the top of one of his towering, gravity-defying piles of paperwork. As he tugged open the top to peer inside, the tantalizing scent of cinnamon rolls wafted out, momentarily blocking out the other less-appealing odors in the station. "Oh man … I'm going to have to do a double workout," he sighed, reaching in to tear off a piece and pop it in his mouth. "As much as I appreciate this, I know it's not the reason you're here. So, out with it. What did you do?"

"How do you know I did anything?"

He gave me a look as he pulled off another piece. "Seriously? You made homemade cinnamon rolls. You must have been up in the middle of the night." Suddenly, his eyes widened. "Oh no. You heard the horse galloping, didn't you?"

I had planned to start with David and then move to the horse galloping, but clearly, that wasn't going to happen. I didn't even need to answer, as he obviously already saw it written on my face.

"Seriously, Charlie," he groaned. "I told you to be careful."

"I'm fine," I said. "Nothing that a couple of uninterrupted nights of sleep won't fix."

He didn't look convinced. "Was there a jack-o'-lantern on your porch, as well?"

I was silent. On second thought, I should have just called him to the house after all.

He closed his eyes. "Charlie, this is getting out of hand. Why didn't you call me?"

"Because I didn't think it was an emergency," I said. "I wasn't going to call you in the middle of the night. I figured I would come in and file a report, like a normal person, and if you thought it was important enough to investigate in person, you'd come by the house at some point."

He threw me a very unhappy look as he pulled another piece off of the cinnamon roll. "Is that the only thing that happened, or do you have something more to tell me?"

I gritted my teeth. Wyle knew me too well. "Have you had a chance to dig into what happened to Abe? Kat's fiancé who was murdered?"

"You mean the love triangle?"

"Yeah, that one."

His eyes narrowed. "I put in a call yesterday, but I had to leave a message. I haven't had a chance to see if the detective called me back yet."

"Well, when the detective does call you back, you might want to ask him a few more questions."

Wyle stared at me for a moment before wiping his hands on a napkin he had brought in with his coffee and fumbling around the cluttered piles of paperwork for his notebook and pen. "All right. I'll bite. What other questions should I ask?"

"Start with whether they know David, the journalist."

Wyle eyed me over his paper. "David the journalist?"

"Yeah, and if they do know him, what's his story?"

"Does David the journalist have a last name?"

"Probably ... give me a minute," I said as I fished out David's card from my bag. I handed it to Wyle, who shot me a skeptical look as he took it.

"David Kaczynski." He pronounced the last name slowly before glancing at me over the card. "I hesitate to ask how you ended up with David Kaczynski's card."

"He gave it to me."

"Oh, so you didn't take it off a bulletin board."

"Do we have a bulletin board somewhere littered with business cards?"

Wyle sighed and pinched the bridge of his nose with his fingers. "Charlie, I swear. When and where did David give you his card?"

"Last night." I paused to take a breath. "At The Tipsy Cow."

Wyle dropped his hand away from his face with a thud. He stared at me. "You were at The Tipsy Cow with him?"

"Yes. He had called me asking me to meet."

"And you said yes?" Wyle's tone went up a notch. "Just like that? Someone you've never met before?"

"Well, to his credit, he pretended to be someone else."

"Who?"

"Ike."

Wyle's eyes went round. "Ike? You thought he was Ike?"

"Not exactly." I squirmed in my seat. Even to my own ears, I sounded ridiculous. No wonder Wyle was constantly harping on me about needing to take my safety more seriously. "He said he was calling on behalf of Ike, who wanted to meet me at The Tipsy Cow."

Wyle was still staring at me. "And you just ... believed him?"

"Why wouldn't I? I figured there was probably a reason why Ike had someone else call me. Remember, the last time I saw him, he went running out of Quote the Raven with no explanation. So, there could have been a good reason for him keeping a low profile."

"Which is why he wanted to meet in a very public place."

"Well, yeah," I admitted. "That did strike me as a little odd."

"But not odd enough to not meet him," Wyle said.

I squirmed in my seat. "Look, do you want to hear about what David told me or not?"

Wyle leaned forward. "Actually, what I'd like to know is why you didn't call me? I could have backed you up. Not to mention you know that I've been trying to pin this guy down for an interview."

"And I planned to persuade him to come in for one," I said. "But in order to do that, I would have to talk to him first. And I didn't want him getting nervous or to scare him away, which might have happened if I had showed up with you."

Wyle lifted his head to stare at the ceiling. "I can't believe this."

"You know how jumpy he's been," I said. "The guy thinks he's being haunted by the Headless Horseman."

"He certainly says that," Wyle said. "What he actually believes is another story."

"Well, regardless of what he believes, he's acting nervous. And nervous people tend to get even more nervous when a cop is around."

Wyle gave me a hard look. "Do you honestly think I would have gone in there with guns blazing or shoving a badge in his face? Give me a little credit. There's a little something called 'undercover work.' Maybe you've heard of it."

My face flushed. "I didn't think of that."

"And that's my point," Wyle said. "That's why you need to call me and tell me before you go off on your own like that."

"Okay, in the future, I'll call you," I said. "Happy?"

Wyle shook his head, muttering to himself as he pulled off another piece of cinnamon roll. "Not particularly, but it will have to do. So, what did David the journalist want?"

"He thinks Ike murdered Abe."

Wyle blinked at me. "Abe? The fiancé?"

"That's the one."

"I thought you said it was a robbery gone bad."

"That's what Kat told me," I said. "David thinks it's all a lie, though, and that Ike was the one who killed him."

Wyle muttered something else under his breath before reaching for another bite. "And why was he telling you this?"

"He wants me to help catch him in a lie or something, so the cops can arrest him."

Wyle stared at me in horror. "Please tell me you didn't agree to that."

"Of course not," I said. "Now *you're* underestimating *me*."

"Like you haven't given me reason to," Wyle said as he picked up the rest of the cinnamon roll. "I think you better start from the beginning. Tell me precisely what David said, start to finish."

So, I did. Wyle took notes between polishing off the cinnamon roll and drinking coffee. When I finished, he didn't immediately say anything. Instead, he took a moment to look through his notes and wipe his fingers on the napkin again.

"Man, this case has taken a bizarre turn," he said, frowning at his notes.

"No question about that."

He glanced up at me. "What was your sense of David? Do you think he's angry enough at Ike to be behind all the pranks?"

"Angry enough to sabotage Ike? Absolutely."

Wyle was closely watching my face. "But ...?"

"I don't see him doing something like this."

"Why not?"

I paused, struggling to put my thoughts in order. "It's too complex. But complex in the wrong way. Yes, he's got this silly elaborate plan to get Ike to confess on tape to a stranger, but this is ... different. There's a lot of planning and coordination involved. Think about it—you'd have to make contacts in all the different towns and know Ike's schedule in order to plan the events accordingly. It would be a lot to manage. And my sense is that's not David's strong point. Not to mention that there would be no way for him to use any of it in an article."

A faint smile touched Wyle's lips. "In other words, he couldn't capitalize on it."

I chuckled. "Something like that."

Wyle made a note as he picked up his coffee. "I feel like these things must be related, but for the life of me, I don't know how. I don't believe in coincidences, so all these people showing up in Redemption at the same time these pranks start occurring doesn't sit well with me. But I'm just not seeing the connection."

"I know. I feel the same. I've been going over and over it, and I can't figure it out, either."

Wyle sat back in his chair, making a slight face as he sipped his coffee. I suspected it had to be cold by that point. "I'm starting to think Ike might be right about something haunting him, after all."

I looked at Wyle in surprise. "You're suddenly a believer in the Headless Horseman?"

He half-smiled. "Maybe not so much that, but something in his past sure seems to be following him around and wreaking havoc not only in his life, but everyone else's."

I hadn't thought about it like that, but it made sense. "I guess now we just have to figure out precisely what that something is."

"And why," Wyle added.

Chapter 12

The phone rang just as I realized I had burnt a batch of my famous chocolate chip cookies.

It was just one of those days.

Even though I had promised Wyle I would back off the case and let him handle it, I couldn't stop thinking about it. He had promised to keep me in the loop as to what he found out, but I had to promise to let him know if either David or Ike contacted me again. "It's not safe, Charlie. Surely you must see that now that you're being targeted."

"It's pranks, Wyle," I said. "A couple of carved pumpkins were left on my porch and the sound of horse galloping woke me up at night. I would hardly call that 'life-threatening.'"

His frown deepened. "You don't know where this is going to go. Sometimes, pranks start out harmless or even childish, but then they escalate."

"It hasn't escalated, though."

"That we know of," Wyle said. "Yes, it's true nothing worse has happened in Redemption, as far as we know. But I haven't been able to track down what happened, if anything, in the other towns. Hence, I need to talk to Ike." He gave me a hard look.

"I get it, I get it," I said. "I'll do what I can to get him to talk to you."

"That would certainly make all our lives easier," Wyle said. "Not just mine, but yours, too. Even though these pranks are fairly harmless right now, do you really want them to keep going?"

He had a point. Despite the fact that I kept telling myself it was just kids or a publicity stunt, there was still something creepy about that smiling jack-o'-lantern waiting for me on the front porch ... never mind the horse galloping.

I came home to discover that Midnight had thrown up his breakfast, so I had to clean that up. Then I couldn't find the file for a new tea client, in which I had taken copious notes about several batches of custom teas I was creating for her. I tore up my entire office looking for it, only to finally locate it in the kitchen under a batch of herbs.

And, to top everything off, I burned a batch of cookies.

Maybe I just needed to go back to bed and try again the next day.

The ringing of the phone cut through my frustrated thoughts. I went to answer it, hoping it wasn't more bad news. Or another hang-up. I had been plagued by those all day, as well, along with several on my answering machine.

"Is this Charlie Kingsley?" The male voice was familiar, but I couldn't place it. I didn't have a lot of men call me—I mostly dealt with their wives, daughters, or girlfriends.

"This is she."

"This is Tad Clark from *The Redemption Times*. I was wondering if you had a moment."

I closed my eyes briefly. Of course. How could I not remember that nasally voice?

Back when I first moved to Redemption, Tad had been a pain in my rear, asking a lot of uncomfortable questions that I had no intention of making the answers to public. I was on the run from an abusive fiancé, after all, and the last thing I needed was publicity.

"No comment."

"I haven't even asked the question yet." The voice was amused.

"The question doesn't matter. I'm not interested in being a part of your story."

"I promise to quote you accurately."

"I'm well aware of all the tricks journalists use to be 'accurate.' Doesn't make it truthful," I said. "Which is why I'm telling you that I have no comment."

"So, does that mean you have or have not had an encounter with the Headless Horseman?"

I went still. Tad was doing a story about these pranks? This couldn't be good. I wondered if Wyle knew about it. "I don't know what you're talking about."

"That's surprising, seeing as how you live in Redemption's most haunted house."

"I don't know what that has to do with anything."

"It appears the Headless Horseman has been targeting local haunted houses and buildings," Tad said. "One person has already been hospitalized from the encounter, and I'm calling to …"

"Hospitalized?" I blurted out. "Who was hospitalized?"

There was a rustling of paper. "Oh, yes. It was a real tragedy. I'll need a minute to consult my notes, but in the meantime, maybe you could answer a few questions for me."

Of all the dirty tricks … was he seriously trying to bribe me with tragic news? My mind raced, going over all the people I knew who lived in haunted homes … especially my elderly clients. What if it was Lee? I should go see her, if it was. Lee was alone in this world, with no kids or husband. She might need help. And this snake wanted to dangle the information in front of me just to get me to give him a quote for his story.

I almost gave in. Almost. But then I realized I could probably figure it out on my own. It might take a little longer, but at least I wouldn't give this so-called "journalist" the satisfaction.

"No dice," I said. "I'll find out on my own. If you'll excuse me, I have some phone calls to make." I could hear Tad's surprised voice begging me to wait as I hung up the phone.

I called Pat, but she wasn't home, so I moved to Wyle, but he wasn't at the station. Argh. I hung up, trying to think about who I could try next, when I heard the distinct sounds of Midnight throwing up in the living room.

Double argh. What a day it was turning out to be. I ran into the living room, only to see Midnight balanced on the coffee table as he hacked away.

"Midnight! What are you doing on the table?"

Midnight turned at the sound of my voice, and just like that, he stopped hacking.

I came toward him. "Are you okay?" He watched me as I approached, blinking his emerald-green eyes. I petted him, running my hands down his body as he stood there licking his whiskers. "Are you sure you're okay?" I asked.

For an answer, he hopped off the coffee table and sauntered into the kitchen, likely to find his spot in the late-afternoon sun to take a nap.

I shook my head and looked down at the coffee table, wanting to make sure he hadn't thrown up anything weird. Other than a few stray cat hairs, I didn't see anything. I picked up the stack of magazines and books just to be sure, but everything looked normal. Well, at least one thing was going my way. It would have been a total disaster if he had thrown up on all that paper.

I put the magazines and books back down and started straightening them. One slipped out, and I saw it was *The True History of Redemption*—the book Ike had wanted. I picked it up and turned it over in my hands, wondering if he had ever gone back to the bookstore to look for it, only to discover someone else had bought it.

Of course, I hadn't bought it for myself, but for him, which made me wonder why I was still hanging onto it. Maybe what I needed to do was take it to the Redemption Inn. And while I was there, I could ask Ike some questions and start getting to the bottom of what was going on. If people were being hospitalized over Headless Horseman pranks, it was high time to put an end to them, once and for all.

I picked up the book and went to fetch my purse.

* * *

"I haven't seen Ike," Nancy said, tugging a hunk of hair behind her ear as she replaced the coffee pot. She seemed a little frazzled, which was unlike her, but in her defense, the Redemption Inn was a lot busier than normal.

"At all?"

"Not at all," she said, collecting the empty platter next to the coffee pot in her other hand. Behind her, in the breakfast room, a burst of laughter roared. "Hold on, I have to refill this." She waved the platter.

"What's going on in there?" I gestured with my head.

"Oh, it's kind of like a PTA, except it's for the local preschool," Nancy said as she hurried into the kitchen. As I waited for her to re-emerge, one of the participants in the meeting came out, an empty cup in hand. When she saw the lack of baked goods, her face fell.

"Nancy is refilling it," I assured her. "She should be out in a minute."

"Oh, good," the woman said, her face relieved. "Not that I need it," she confessed patting her hip. "But you can't beat Nancy's gingersnaps."

"No, you can't," I agreed as Nancy reappeared, platter over-flowing with cookies. The woman helped herself to one, then refilled her coffee cup and headed back into the breakfast room.

"So, Ike has managed to slip in and out without you noticing him," I said.

Nancy let out a bark of laughter. "Slip in and out? No, you don't understand. He hasn't been here at all."

I looked at her in confusion. "You mean he checked out?"

She shook her head so vehemently, her straw-like hair dislodged from behind her ears and swung in front of her face. Impatiently, she tucked it back again. "No, his stuff is still in his room. But no Ike."

"How can you be sure he isn't coming and going when you aren't around?"

"Because his room hasn't been used," she said.

"Are you sure?"

"Positive," she confirmed. "Nothing has been touched. His bed, the towels, his belongings. His papers are still in the same pile on the table, and his clothes are hanging in the closet."

I looked at her in bewilderment. "He hasn't been in his room at all? For how long?"

She chewed on her lip. "The last time I saw him was when he came running in like a bat out of hell before flying right back out. That was three days ago, I think."

"What about his car? Or does he have a car?" It suddenly occurred to me I wasn't sure how Ike traveled between cities. I had just assumed he drove.

"Still in the parking lot. Hasn't moved."

Where could Ike have gone for three days without his car? Where had he been sleeping? And bathing? Was he wearing the same clothes? And what about his research?

Even more than that, what could he possibly have been doing for three days, where no one would notice him? Redemption was a fairly small town. It seemed unbelievable to think that no one had seen him for days.

Nancy leaned closer. "You don't think the Headless Horseman got him, do you?"

A trickle of unease drifted down my spine. "Why would you say that?"

She stared at me like I had lost my mind. "Well, because of what's been going on, of course. The jack-o'-lanterns being left on porches and the sound of the horse galloping at night. Seems like maybe he was whisked away by the Headless Horseman, doesn't it?" She laughed, and I forced a smile, but in my mind's eye, I was seeing Ike's terrified face.

I think I'm being haunted by the Headless Horseman.

It sounded ridiculous when we were standing in the middle of a bookstore. But now, I was starting to wonder.

"Charlie! Is that you?"

I felt a sinking in the pit of my stomach as I plastered a smile on my face and turned around. David was standing there, grinning at me. "Hi, David."

"I was just thinking of you. I'm so glad to run into you."

"Redemption is a small town," I said when I couldn't think of an appropriate answer.

An older couple was moving toward me, suitcases in hand, and I realized David and I were blocking the check-in desk, so I moved to the side, closer to the breakfast room. David followed, clearly thinking I was trying to have a more private conversation with him. "Are you meeting Ike?" he asked, his voice barely containing his excitement.

"No, I'm afraid not."

David's face fell. "But you were asking about him."

I stared at him. "You were spying on me?"

His expression was horrified. "No! I wasn't trying to spy. I just heard you say his name, and I thought ... I assumed ..." He seemed so distressed, I almost felt sorry for him, but then I remembered how he had been skulking around the first time I had been at the inn looking for Ike, too. Suddenly, I wondered just how innocent he was.

"If you heard me say his name, you must have also heard that Nancy hasn't seen him," I said.

He furrowed his brow. "What do you mean, Nancy hasn't seen him? Maybe she just wasn't around when he's come in and out."

"Maybe. But according to her, his room hasn't been used in days." I gave him a hard look. "Are you sure you don't know anything about this?"

His eyes widened. "What are you saying? I had something to do with his apparent disappearance?"

I crossed my arms across my chest. "I didn't say that. But don't you think it's suspicious that Ike has disappeared shortly after you showed up?"

David sputtered. "I don't know what you're talking about."

Something caught my attention from the corner of my eye. I turned to see Louise standing near the coffee, her thick blonde hair loose around her shoulders. She wore a blue silk blouse that perfectly matched her eyes. As attractive as she was, she wasn't nearly as good-looking as her brother Jesse had been. Her face was a little rounder and her lips not as full. She was refilling her cup and watching us intently, that same smug smile on her lips.

All my senses were on high alert. Even though it made no sense, there was something about her that was making me very uncomfortable. For the life of me, I couldn't figure out what.

I deliberately turned away from Louise and back to David, although I could still feel her eyes crawling down my neck. "This is why assumptions are so dangerous."

His look was wary. "I don't know what you mean."

"It's just that you've made a lot of assumptions about Ike. I'm not saying you're wrong … maybe he really did kill Abe. But maybe there's something else going on."

David stared at me before taking a step away. "He got to you, didn't he?"

"Got to me? What are you talking about?"

"What do you think?" David's tone was bitter. "That's the problem with psychopaths. They're so charming, the average person doesn't even realize they're being manipulated."

"So now Ike is a psychopath?" I shook my head. "David, I think you need to get a grip. This obsession you have with him … it's not healthy."

He laughed, but there was no humor in it. "I'm obsessed? I'm the only one who sees Ike for what he is! But it doesn't matter what I say. I keep warning people and warning people, and it's only when it's too late that they realize the truth."

The conversation was getting more awkward the longer I was in it. I eased backward a step, thinking I might need to reconsider my earlier thoughts on David. At this point, with the unhealthy glitter in his eyes, I wouldn't put anything past him, including him being behind the pranks. "If that's the case—that you have warned people, and they refuse to listen until it's too late—you might want to reconsider your approach. Maybe you need to do or say something a little differently to get people's attention."

David wasn't impressed with my gentle critique. "Man, you have it bad, don't you?" The look he gave me was full of pity. "I truly thought you were different … that you could see through his lies, but …" he held his hands up, palms facing the ceiling. "You're just like all the rest."

"David, I'm saying this to you as a person concerned for your welfare," I said, my tone firm. "Please get yourself some help."

But David wasn't listening. He had already turned away, shaking his head in disgust. "Thanks for nothing."

"Well, I do hope you find what you're looking for," I offered.

"No thanks to you," he spat as he walked away.

While a big part of me was relieved as I watched him go, since I wouldn't have to worry about him bugging me to help with his ridiculous schemes any longer, another part of me almost felt sorry for him. I wished I would have been more successful in getting through to him, so he could recognize that his obsession wasn't healthy. Even if he was right about Ike, which was certainly possible, I feared his fixation was causing him to walk a very dark path.

Which led to yet another part of me that felt the need to tell someone what was going on with David. It was possible he wasn't stable. But who would I tell? Wyle? While it would be a good thing to give him a heads-up, I wasn't sure what, if anything, he could do. It's not like being obsessed with someone or something was against the law, in and of itself. And as far as I knew, David hadn't done anything other than want to secretly record Ike. In some states, it was against the law to record someone without their knowledge, so that could actually be a crime. But how dangerous was it, really? Was it even possible to arrest someone on suspicion of recording someone without their knowledge?

Yeah, that seemed pretty weak.

I could still feel eyes on the back of my neck, and I turned to see Louise still standing there, watching me, an unreadable expression on her face. How long had she been there? The entire time? What was her problem?

My intention was to walk away, but instead, I found myself striding over to her. "Did you need something from me, Louise?" I asked her, keeping my voice pleasant.

Her china-blue eyes narrowed. "Other than you leaving Redemption? No."

"That's why you're not in your meeting? Because you needed to tell me that, yet again?" I nodded toward the open door.

The smug smile returned, playing along her lips. "No. I was just enjoying the show."

That uneasy feeling crept through me again. "What show?"

She gestured with her head toward where David had disappeared. "The one that will get you out of my hair once and for all."

"What are you talking about, Louise?" My voice was exasperated, but that uneasy feeling was stronger. What on Earth did she know that I didn't?

Her smile was brittle. "You should be more careful about the friends you keep. Someone might get the wrong impression."

I put my hands on my hips. "What is THAT supposed to mean?"

"Just a little friendly advice," Louise said before turning on her heel and walking into the breakfast room.

I stood there for a moment, gathering my thoughts. She had to be talking about David. As far as I could tell, she had only seen me with him, not Ike or Kat. Did that mean there was something more troubling about David after all?

I had been getting a bad feeling from him since the beginning, but I thought it was more about his preoccupation with Ike. Maybe there was more to it after all.

From where I was standing, I could see partly into the breakfast room, and I found myself peering inside. I couldn't see Louise from the angle where I was, but I did see Claire, the very first person I'd met in Redemption and one of my best friends, other than Pat. She must have felt my eyes on her, because she turned her head slightly, her strawberry-blonde hair coming loose from its ponytail and trailing into her face. She smiled at me, her hazel eyes crinkling, and threw me a tiny wave.

I waved back, thinking I would need to call her the next day to find out more about the meeting and to see if she knew what Louise was talking about.

Chapter 13

"Have you seen the paper today?" Pat asked the moment I picked up the phone.

"Not yet," I yawned. I had overslept and was still groggy. Finally, I had gotten a decent night's sleep. I tucked the phone between my ear and shoulder as I turned on the stove and moved the tea kettle over. Midnight wound himself around my ankles, reminding me that along with being late with my tea, I was late with his breakfast.

"What, did I wake you?"

"No, I was up," I said. "Barely, but I was up."

Pat's question was ping-ponging in my brain. Whatever she was referring to in the paper should be important, but my brain was too fuzzy and thick with sleep to figure it out.

"Do you have tea?"

"Getting there." I opened one of the cabinets to fish out my teapot. "Are you angling for an invitation?"

"Once you see what's in the paper, you'll want me there," Pat said. "I'll be right over."

I hung up the phone and went to check on the bakery goods I had on hand. I knew I still had muffins for sure, and I thought there might be some banana bread, as well ...

I froze. *Have you seen the paper today?*

Oh no. Tad. He had called me for a quote. I had just about forgotten about him, having been so consumed with David and Louise.

He must have printed something dreadful. Crap. I figured I'd better go see.

I hurried out of the kitchen, ignoring Midnight's surprised and none-too-happy meow, and over to the front door. I shoved my feet into a pair of tennis shoes, although I didn't bother to tie them, and headed out to fetch the paper.

There was a bite to the air that cut through the thin sweat-shirt I had tossed over my sleeping outfit. I crossed my arms across my chest and half-jogged to the bottom of the driveway. At least the cold air helped clear the fog out of my brain. I had a feeling I was going to need a clear head.

It was too cold to unroll the paper outside, and by the time I got inside, the tea kettle was singing, and Midnight was sitting impatiently at the kitchen door, his tail twitching as his emer-ald-green eyes bored into me.

By the time I got the tea brewing and Midnight fed, I figured Pat would be by in a minute or two, so I might as well put out the muffins, the last couple of pieces of banana bread, and a plate of homemade dog biscuits for Tiki. I had the table set when I heard the front door open.

"In the kitchen," I called out.

"I wouldn't imagine you were anywhere else," Pat said as Tiki came running in to greet me, nails clicking on the tile floor. "No jack-o'-lantern, I see. Or did you throw it away?"

"No, not today, at least," I said, realizing I had been so pre-occupied with whatever lies Tad likely printed about me that I had forgotten about the jack-o'-lanterns.

Pat's eyebrow raised. "Not today? You've had more?"

I let out a breath as I ran a hand through my wild, tangled mop of hair. I had forgotten to tell Pat not only about the sec-ond jack-o'-lantern, but the sound of a galloping horse waking me up, too. "Oh man. I've got so much to catch you up on. But before we do that, I have to know … what dreadful thing has Tad published about me today?"

"Tad?" Pat frowned as she moved to sit at the kitchen table. I had already set out mugs and plates, so I just needed to bring over the teapot and pour us both a cup. "Why would Tad be writing a story about you?"

"I have no idea. All I know is he called me for a quote." I finished pouring the tea and sat down across from her.

Pat reached down to scoop up Tiki, who was eager to settle into her lap. She was wearing a bright-orange sweater with a jack-o'-lantern face on it and matching orange ribbons in her fur. Her little black eyes were bright, too, as she looked longingly at the dog biscuits. "What did he want a quote about?"

"We didn't get that far," I said.

Pat looked confused. "You didn't get that far?" She absently reached for a dog biscuit.

"It's a long story. I have a lot to catch you up on. But first, if it wasn't Tad, then what's in the paper?"

"You still haven't looked?"

"No, I had to get ready for you."

"Oh, well. I'm glad you got your priorities sorted out." Pat picked up her mug. "So, it appears our Sleepy Hollow visitor has been murdered."

"What?" In my shock, I dropped my mug, the brown liquid sloshing over the side. "Ike was murdered?" In my mind, I saw him standing in the Quote the Raven bookstore, his eyes full of excitement as he showed me the book he discovered. I could already feel the grief pressing against my chest.

Pat frowned again. "No, that wasn't the name. It was the other one."

"Other one? Not Ike?" Now it was my turn to frown. "Was it Kat?" The grief pressing against my chest turned to dread. Did this mean David was right about Ike after all? That he really was a psychopath who had first killed Kat's fiancé, and now Kat herself?

Pat was staring at me. "Kat. Who's Kat? Oh, that's right. Ike's girlfriend. How many people from Sleepy Hollow are here in Redemption right now anyway?"

"So it's not Kat?"

She shook her head. "No, it's like Dan or Daemon or something."

"David."

"Yes, David." Pat sat back, obviously relieved that we'd finally gotten the name right. But then, she immediately furrowed her brow. "How did you know that?"

"I also know he's a journalist investigating Ike," I said a little smugly.

Pat's eyebrows shot up. "What? Investigating him for what?"

"Murder."

"*Murder*?" Her eyes bugged out. "You better start from the beginning."

I quickly filled her in on the details. "But what I really want to know is what happened to David?"

She screwed up her face. "I think he was found dead in his hotel room."

"What?"

"Yeah, he was stabbed or something. Where's your paper?"

I fetched it from the counter and unrolled it. It wasn't difficult to find the article, as it was right on the front page. *Headless Horseman in Redemption?*

"Oh geez," I muttered, quickly skimming the article. My eyes widened when I discovered what had killed David. I looked up and saw Pat watching me with a knowing look in her eyes.

"David was killed by a pumpkin-carving knife?"

Pat nodded and reached for a muffin. "I told you that you'd want me here."

"But ..." I stared down at the newspaper and swallowed hard. "It's got to be a coincidence. I mean, a knife is a knife, right? Just because you can use it to carve a pumpkin doesn't mean that's what it was used for before. And it doesn't mean that whoever killed David was responsible for carving the jack-o'-lanterns left on our porches, either."

"No, it doesn't," Pat agreed. "But still ... it's creepy."

I reached for a muffin, more for something to do as my stomach was so twisted up in knots, I didn't think I could eat anything. I kept remembering the feeling of someone hanging around outside my house in the middle of the night. If that person had been carrying a knife ... I didn't want to think about it. "Yeah, it is."

"Although you're right ... it's probably not the Headless Horseman," Pat said. "As it sounds like David's head was intact."

I gave her a look. "You're horrible."

"Well, it's true. If there was no head and a jack-o'-lantern left in its place, that would seem more like the work of the Headless Horseman."

"Or someone who was trying to frame the Headless Horseman," I suggested.

"That's also true," Pat said, rubbing her chin. "If you can pin a murder on a ghost, that would be a great way to get away with it. Maybe that's why whoever killed David used a pumpkin-carving knife."

"Again, you can use any kind of knife to carve a pumpkin," I said. "The paper is trying to make this sound as lurid as possible to sell copies. Whatever happened to David probably has nothing to do with the jack-o'-lanterns."

"Probably," Pat agreed. "Although ..." she paused and cocked her head. "Wyle may not think so."

I sighed. "Yeah. I'm going to have to listen to another lecture."

"I wonder who the suspects are," Pat said, gesturing toward the paper.

"Wait, they have a suspect?" I glanced back down at the article.

"Yeah, there's a witness, I guess, and police are following up."

I frowned. "A witness. But I thought he was killed in his hotel room."

"Maybe someone saw the killer go in or out of the room."

"Maybe," I said, but I was starting to get a bad feeling. I could see Louise's smug smile as she watched me and David. I wasn't sure if she had heard every word, but it had been clear David was upset with me.

Had Louise said something to the police? Even if she had, she surely would have seen David go upstairs and me leave the hotel.

Something wasn't right.

The phone rang at that moment, jerking me out of my thoughts and causing me to spill my tea again.

Pat noticed. "Are you sure you're alright? You seem awfully jumpy."

"I'll be fine," I said, getting up to answer the phone. "It's just this case. It's giving me the creeps."

"No question it's a creepy one," Pat said.

I picked up the phone. "Charlie?" It was Wyle.

My stomach squeezed into an even tighter knot. There was something in his voice that didn't sound right. "I'm fine," I said quickly. "Not even a jack-o'-lantern on my porch today."

"I'm not calling about that," he said. His voice was oddly formal. "I have to ask you to come down to the station."

All my senses went on high alert. "Why?"

"To ask you a few questions about David Kaczynski."

My stomach squeezed even tighter. I was having trouble breathing. All I could see was Louise's smug face in my mind's eye. "Why?"

He paused. "There's a witness who claims they saw you with David last night. Before he died."

"Oh, that Louise," I snapped. "Wyle, it's not what you think. I was ..."

"Charlie, not now," he interrupted. "Just come down to the station, okay? And we'll clear it all up."

My shoulders slumped over. It was like all the air left my body. I told him I'd be down within the hour and hung up.

Pat was staring at me, her mouth hanging open. "What was that all about?"

I started to run my hands through my hair. It was a tangled mess. I didn't have time to take a shower, so I was going to pull it up in a ponytail. "Apparently, it's me," I answered. "I'm the suspect."

Chapter 14

"Wyle, you must know I had nothing to do with David's death," I said as soon as he approached me in the station.

Wyle not only shot me a look, but he held up a hand, too, clearly communicating that I should be quiet. "We just have a few questions," he said, his voice formal. "If you'll follow me, I'll get the interview started."

Interview started? Oh, this didn't sound good.

Pat had wanted me to call a lawyer, but I told her I didn't think it was necessary. "It's Wyle," I said. "He can't possibly suspect me in David's death."

Pat's expression was serious. "Charlie, you don't know what they have. People get railroaded all the time by the cops."

"This is Wyle we're talking about," I said. "I can't imagine him railroading me. And Redemption's is a small-town police department. They don't do things like that here."

Pat frowned. "You'd be surprised," she said darkly.

I wanted to ask her more about that, but I didn't have much time before I needed to be at the station.

When I wouldn't call a lawyer, Pat wanted to come with me, but I refused, thinking that would be too weird. "Besides, if this is an actual official interview, they probably won't even let you in the room," I said. "They don't let friends in—only lawyers and guardians."

Pat's frown deepened. "I don't like this at all, Charlie. Call me the moment you're done."

I agreed, but I still thought she was overreacting. For goodness' sake, a lot of the police officers knew me. I helped them with their cases. They wouldn't try and frame me for something I didn't do.

And what proof could they have? Louise watching me talk to David? Even if she told the police we were arguing, that still didn't prove anything. And someone surely must have seen me leave the hotel.

But now that I was at the station, and Wyle was definitely not acting like his normal self, I was starting to get a little concerned. Maybe Pat was right after all, and I should have called a lawyer.

Wyle led me to one of the interrogation rooms, asked me if I wanted anything to drink, which I declined, and told me to have a seat … that he'd back in a moment. I sat down in one of the plastic chairs, nervously glancing at the mirror.

I wondered who was watching me.

After a moment, Wyle came back in carrying a file, tape recorder, and a cup of coffee. He sat down across from me, smoothed his shirt down in front of him, and placed all the items on the table. "Do you mind if I record?" he asked, picking up the device.

I eyed it. "Should I be calling a lawyer?"

Something flickered across his face. "That's up to you. Do you feel like you need to call a lawyer?"

"I don't know. Do you feel like you need to record the interview?"

"It's standard procedure."

I looked directly at him. "Am I under arrest?"

He stared back at me, something unreadable in his gaze. "You're not under arrest. We just have a few questions, is all. You're under no obligation to answer them, and you can leave at any time. If you want to call a lawyer, that is your right. Do you want to?"

I chewed on my bottom lip. "What are the questions you want to ask me?"

"Just where you were last night."

"If that's the case, then why all of this?" I made a sweeping gesture with my hand, indicating the tape recorder, the room, and whoever was watching on the other side of the mirror.

"Just procedure," he said. "We want to make sure we're doing everything by the book. Now ..." He picked up the recorder. "Do I have your permission to record?"

I didn't like any of it, but I still felt like I had nothing to hide. I also wanted to know what the cops thought they had on me, and I didn't think that would happen unless I gave Wyle the permission he was asking for. "Fine."

He clicked it on, then spoke into it the date, time, and my name. He placed it on the table between us, then opened his notebook. "Okay, so let's start with where you were last night."

"Home."

"Any witnesses to that?"

"Midnight."

He glanced up at me. "Your cat?"

"That's him."

He didn't look amused. "Anyone else?"

"No, it was a pretty quiet night."

"What did you do?"

"Made dinner, took a bath, read a book, and went to bed early."

He nodded and jotted down some notes. "What about earlier? Had you gone anywhere?"

"Why, yes. I had gone to the Redemption Inn that afternoon." I sat back in my chair. "But I expect you already know that."

He didn't take the bait. "What time was that?"

I screwed up my face. "I think it was around four or so. I wasn't really paying attention to the time. I didn't think I would have to account for it later."

"How long were you there?"

"Not long. Ten, maybe fifteen minutes. Maybe a little longer."

"Why were you there?"

"I was looking for someone."

Wyle glanced up at me, his eyes narrowing slightly. "Who?"

"Just someone. But it doesn't matter because he wasn't there."

"Everything matters in a murder investigation," Wyle said.

"Yes, but I didn't have anything to do with the murder, so I don't see why who I was looking for matters."

"Humor me," Wyle said. "It may not mean anything, but it could also be important."

I exhaled hard through my nose. I told myself it wasn't a big deal, and that he probably already knew. But still, I found myself reluctant to tell him. "I was trying to track down Ike."

"Ike Krane?"

"Yes."

"Why were you trying to track him down?"

"Because I want to get to the bottom of whatever is going on in this town," I said. "Whoever is behind these pranks is getting out of hand. People are getting hurt. It's got to stop."

"By 'pranks,' you mean …"

"The jack-o'-lanterns being left on porches and the sounds of a horse galloping at night."

"Who is getting hurt?"

I slumped over, realizing I had forgotten to ask Pat. Or Nancy. She might have known, as well, but David had distracted me. "I'm not sure."

Wyle gave me a curious look. "You sounded sure."

"Well, it was that stupid journalist who said something," I said.

"David?"

"No. Tad."

Wyle looked surprised. "Tad? From *The Redemption Times*?"

"The one and same."

"What does he have to do with this?"

"He called me yesterday and wanted a quote for a story he's writing."

Wyle looked even more surprised. "What story?"

"I assume it's about the pranks."

"You assume?"

I sighed. "We didn't get far, but he was talking about the Headless Horseman, and how someone was hospitalized after an encounter with him."

"Did he mention who?"

"Only if I promised to answer his questions," I said. "And I wouldn't, so no."

A ghost of a smile touched Wyle's lips, and he dipped his head to focus on his notes. "Okay, was it after this call that you went to the Redemption Inn?"

"Yes. To see if I could get answers from Ike once and for all."

"In other words, you decided to involve yourself in an investigation," Wyle said. His tone was neutral, but I could see a muscle jump in his jaw.

"I'm already involved, seeing as how my house has been targeted," I said. "There's no 'involving myself.' Plus, I've already had a couple of conversations with Ike, which you already know about, so I figured he would be more likely to talk to me."

"I see," Wyle said. "So, you went to the Redemption Inn, but you were unable to find him ..."

"No one has been able to find him," I interrupted.

Wyle raised an eyebrow. "What do you mean?"

"He's disappeared. Have you talked to Nancy?"

"What does Nancy say?"

"According to her, not only has she not seen Ike for the past few days, but it appears his room hasn't been used at all."

"What does that mean, it hasn't been used?"

"Just what I said. His bed hasn't been slept in, and he hasn't used the bathroom. Nancy said it doesn't even look like he's touched his papers or changed clothes."

Wyle made a note. "Do you have any idea where he is?"

"If I knew that, I would have gone there instead of the Redemption Inn," I said.

That faint smile touched his lips again. "Fair enough. So, you spoke to Nancy. Then what?"

"David overheard me ask about Ike and assumed I was there to see him. But I told him Ike wasn't there. And we ended up … well, 'arguing' is too strong of a word. But David was pretty upset with me."

"You argued over Ike not being there?" Wyle's expression was skeptical.

I sighed. "Not exactly. He's just so … obsessive about Ike. It was like he didn't believe me when I said Ike hadn't been in his room."

"You told him that?"

"Well, yeah. I didn't think it was a secret. And I certainly didn't think David was going to be killed. But it was just …" I paused, trying to figure out how to say what I was going to without it sounding, well, bad. It was more than just speaking ill of the dead. I was sitting in a police station clearly under some suspicion, and just a few hours before the murder, I had told David he needed help.

Wyle didn't say anything, just let me gather my thoughts. It occurred to me that maybe it really was a good time to ask for a lawyer, but then I figured I was already in the middle of the story, so I might as well finish it.

"There was something … disturbing about David's fixation on Ike," I said. "I didn't think it was healthy, and I told David that. He didn't take it well."

"What did he do?"

"He got upset. Told me I was under Ike's spell, whatever that means. He's convinced that Ike is the psychopath in all of this, and we're all his gullible victims."

"Then what?"

"Then nothing. He left, and I went home." I paused and sat straight up. "Actually, that wasn't it. I talked to Louise."

"Louise Sanders?"

"Yes. She was at some sort of PTO meeting or something. Claire was there, too. You could talk to her."

Wyle made a note. I gave myself a mental pat on the back for working Claire in. Claire would have my back. I was sure of it.

"So, what happened with Louise?"

"Not much. But she did seem to infer that maybe I shouldn't be seen talking to David, for some reason." I tilted my head. "I suspect she's the one who told you I had gotten into a fight with David hours before he was killed."

"We're not at liberty to discuss an open case," Wyle said.

"Yes, of course not. But if I were you, I might ask Louise a thing or two about what she knows. In hindsight, she was acting almost like she knew something would happen to David."

"What do you mean?"

"Exactly what I said. She warned me about the company I was keeping. Why would she possibly care if I was seen having a heated conversation with a journalist unless she knew something might happen to that journalist and suspicion would fall on me?"

"I'll keep that in mind," Wyle said drily. "So, to be clear, did you see David again that night?"

"No." My voice was firm. "That was the last time I saw him."

He glanced at me, his expression unreadable. "Okay, then." He flipped his notebook closed. "Thanks for coming in."

I gave him a double take. "That's it?"

"For now. But I advise you to not go anywhere, or if you do, let us know."

"Okay," I said, getting to my feet. I snuck a peek at the mirror, still wondering who was behind it. Were they satisfied with what they'd heard? Were they convinced of my innocence?

Or was something else going on?

I kept thinking of Pat's words. *You'd be surprised.*

The uneasy feeling settled around me like an old shawl. Had I gotten myself into something way over my head?

Chapter 15

I was too out of sorts to go home, so I went to Aunt May's Diner instead. Sue, one of the long-term waitresses, let me use the house phone to call Pat before seating me in a booth in the back. She must have seen something on my face that indicated I wanted privacy. I kept my head down, as Aunt May's still had a healthy breakfast crowd, and I didn't want to catch anyone's eye. The last thing I felt like doing was talking to anyone.

I immediately ordered coffee, which caused Sue's eyebrows to raise slightly, but she brought it over without a word. Normally, I had tea, but I hadn't brought any of mine with me, and I didn't think I could bear the store-bought type right then. Instead, I doctored my coffee with plenty of cream and sugar. I figured it would help with the wired feeling.

Wyle had walked me down the hallway, reiterating that I should stay close to home in case they had any more questions.

"Fine," I had muttered in response. Even though I had a feeling Wyle had no choice but to treat me as a "person of interest," it still felt like a knife twisting in my gut. I wondered if our old, comfortable relationship in which we mutually respected each other and what we brought to an investigation was salvageable or completely dead.

He pressed his lips together before leaning forward slightly. "I'll call you later," he said under his breath before turning away.

It happened so fast, I wasn't sure if I had imagined it or not. I stole another look at him, but all I could see was his broad back, striding away from me.

I turned and headed out of the police station.

Pat arrived slightly out of breath and faster than I expected. She must have been sitting there ready to walk out the door the moment I called.

She slid into the booth in front of me, waving at Sue before peering at my cup. "Oh, coffee." She eyed me. "That's not a good sign."

I cupped my hands around the mug trying to absorb the warmth from it. "I don't know what to think."

Sue came over with the coffee pot, her eyebrows raised in question. "Yeah, give me what she's having," Pat said. Sue flipped over the empty cup and filled it before topping off mine. "Do you know what you want?"

"Just coffee," I said. My stomach was in too many knots to think about food.

Pat frowned at me. "Give us a minute to decide."

Sue gave Pat a knowing look and left.

"You have to eat," Pat said. "Even if it's something like toast."

I sighed and poured a little more cream into my coffee. "I know. I'm just not hungry."

"You have to try," Pat directed.

"I will," I said. Pat made a face at me as she reached for the cream, and it suddenly occurred to me there was no sign of Tiki.

"Tiki is home?"

"For now," Pat said. "I know Sue says she doesn't care if I bring her in here, but I wasn't sure how long I would be, and it seemed better to leave her home." She took a sip of coffee, eyeing me over the rim. "So, how bad was it?"

"Bad," I answered.

She shook her head. "Was Wyle there?"

I rubbed my face. "He was the one who did the interview."

"Oh boy," Pat said. "You better start from the beginning."

I did, only taking breaks when Sue came by, first to see if we were ready to order and second to bring the food. By then, I had decided Pat was right, and I ordered toast, bacon, and home fries. Pat chose the French toast special.

I not only filled Pat in on what happened at the station, but also on what had been happening over the past couple of days.

"This is nuts," Pat said when I took a breath. She waved at my food. "Eat. Before it gets too cold."

I took a bite of toast and bacon, which was more lukewarm than cold. But it still tasted fine, though that could have been more about my appetite waking up—maybe unburdening myself to Pat was enough to calm me and unwind the knot in my stomach.

"So, the cops didn't tell you why they wanted to interview you?" Pat asked.

I shook my head and took another bite. "I assume it's because of whatever Louise told them," I said, trying to talk around my food. "I figured she made my exchange with David seem worse than it was."

Pat jabbed at her French toast. "One of these days, I'm going to have a talk with her. This … vendetta, or whatever she has against you, is getting ridiculous. Yes, it's unfortunate that her brother hasn't been in touch with her, but that's hardly your fault."

"I don't think talking to her is going to make a difference," I said. "She's made up her mind, and I don't see anything changing it."

"Well, someone needs to at least try," Pat said, glowering at her plate. "She's being childish."

"That may be, but it's not going to help me with the police now."

"It might, if she tells the cops the truth. That whatever she saw wasn't as big of a deal as she's making it out to be."

"Maybe," I said. "But maybe what the cops should do is ask more questions. There were plenty of people around, including Nancy. I'm sure they would get a more … measured description of what happened."

"Yeah, you do have to wonder why they didn't do that," Pat said.

"Unless they wanted to get my take first," I said. "Or maybe they did talk to other people, but they still wanted to hear from me, as well."

"I suppose. But this idea that you were somehow involved with David's death is absurd. I don't care if you two were screaming at each other in the lobby. There's no way you would have snuck back into the hotel and stabbed David." Pat was doing her own stabbing at her food as she talked, and I winced. "Wyle should know better."

"Well, in his defense, I got the sense it wasn't his idea," I said.

Pat threw one final glare at her plate before putting her fork down and picking up her coffee cup. "Okay. All that aside, I get why they talked to you. Of course they would want to hear what you had to say, as you were talking to David a few hours before he died. But the way they're going about it is ... troubling."

I cocked my head. "Do you think they have something more than just Louise?"

Pat stared at me. "Don't you?"

I felt a cold shiver run through me, and I picked up my coffee, as well. "I guess now that you say it, yeah, I do. Although I can't imagine what it could be."

"I know." Pat's expression was brooding, and we were silent for a moment. I took another bite of my food, although I was rapidly losing my appetite again.

"Do you think it might have something to do with Ike?" Pat asked.

"What do you mean?"

"Well, he seems to be the common denominator," Pat said. "The pranks started when he arrived, and according to Ike, that's a regular occurrence. David is here because of Ike. And Ike has now conveniently disappeared just when his nemesis happened to be murdered."

"We don't know if David is Ike's nemeses," I said.

"David is trying to get Ike arrested for murder," Pat said. "That seems to be pretty classic behavior of a nemesis."

"I suppose when you put it that way, it makes sense," I said. "But nemesis or not, are you saying Ike killed David?"

Pat shrugged. "Seems like a pretty decent motive. David is trying to ruin Ike's life, so Ike decides to get rid of David first."

"Yes, but that assumes David actually *could* ruin Ike's life," I said. "Sure, he was trying to, but 'trying' is the operative word. As far as I could tell, he didn't have anything but a bunch of nutty plans that were destined to fail."

"Yes, but Ike might not know that," Pat argued. "Maybe Ike thought David had something on him."

I stared at Pat in disbelief. "And you think Ike *thinking* that would be enough to kill him? Doesn't that seem a little drastic to you?"

Pat eyed me. "We're not talking about us. We're talking about someone neither of us knows. How do we know what Ike is capable of or not?"

"Yes, but ..." I thought about Ike—how in his eagerness to talk about ghosts, his hair would fall into his eyes and his glasses would slip down on his nose. "I don't see it," I finally said flatly.

"You don't see him killing Abe or David?"

"Neither," I said. "We're talking about a guy who thinks the Headless Horseman is following him around, for Pete's sake. This is not a hardened criminal."

Pat studied me for a moment. "Oh, so that's what's going on," she said, almost like she was talking to herself.

"What?"

"Now it all makes sense," she continued, nodding to herself. She sat back in her seat, still holding her coffee cup.

"What are you talking about?" My voice was impatient.

"You have feelings for Ike."

"What? No, I don't."

"And that's why Wyle is being so stubborn ... because he sees it, too."

"You are way off," I said. "There is nothing going on between Ike and me."

"I'm sure there isn't," Pat said. "But that doesn't mean you don't *want* something to happen."

"I don't want anything to happen with anyone," I insisted. "I'm not interested in any sort of relationship."

Pat gave me a look before leaning forward slightly. "Honey, you can lie to yourself, but you can't lie to me." Her voice was firm. "You and Wyle have been doing this dance for a while now, and now, there's someone new in town, which has changed everything."

"No, it hasn't," I said, my voice a little too high. "Nothing has changed."

Suddenly, Pat's eyes went wide. "Wait a second. You were going on a date with Wyle when you met Ike, weren't you?"

"It wasn't a date."

"Oh, now this is *really* making sense," Pat said. "You and Wyle were getting ready to take it to another level, but for whatever reason, you're afraid of commitment. Enter Ike. And, just like that, Wyle has a rival, and you have an excuse to not take any action with either relationship."

"You're delusional," I said, but my voice didn't sound so convinced.

Pat raised her eyebrow. "Am I?"

I had no answer, so I made a face at her. Truthfully, what she said hit a little closer to home than I was comfortable with, and I found myself shifting in my seat.

Was it possible I was more open to Ike's flirtations because I wanted to put up a wall between Wyle and me? Had I sensed that something was shifting between us, so I deliberately encouraged Ike in some way to stop it?

The idea that I might be capable of such passive-aggressive behavior didn't sit well with me at all. I always prided myself on being honest and forthright with all my relationships, and the thought of doing that to Wyle was upsetting.

"Although there's another explanation," Pat broke in. She had been watching my face closely and maybe decided she had pushed me far enough for the moment.

"What?"

"It's the Headless Horseman's fault."

"You think the Headless Horseman killed David?" I asked.

"Well, he was stabbed with a pumpkin-carving knife," Pat said. "But also, Ike has disappeared. Maybe the Headless Horseman really HAS been following him all this time, and he finally got him."

"If that were true, why would he then kill David?"

"Maybe he didn't like David either," Pat said. "Or maybe he just likes to kill people."

"Or ... maybe the Headless Horseman was trying to help Ike," I said.

Pat's eyes lit up. "Oooh. Now you're talking. I like that idea. The Headless Horseman is actually a friend of Ike's, not a foe."

"Yes, so he was behind all those pranks and hauntings in order to help him sell his book, and when David showed up, he decided to take care of the problem by making Ike disappear and killing David," I said.

"I think you're on to something," Pat said. "You need to tell Wyle your theory."

I started to say I would have to see if Wyle actually called like he promised when something in the corner of my eye caught my attention. For a moment, I could only stare, trying to process what I was seeing.

"Earth to Charlie," Pat said, waving a hand in front of my face.

I blinked and focused on Pat. "Sorry," I said. "I just can't believe it. Louise is sitting over there with Kat."

Pat's eyes went wide. "*Louise* is here?" She craned her neck around. "The nerve of her. I should go give her a piece of my mind."

"Hang on," I said, reaching over to touch her hand. "You don't understand. She's over there with *Kat*. Ike's girlfriend."

Pat turned to face me, her mouth hanging open. "Wait. *That* Kat? Why is Louse with her? How did they even meet?"

"I don't know," I said, sliding out of the booth. "But I have some questions for Kat that I'd like to get answered."

"I'd like to get some answers, too," Pat said grimly while following me out of the booth. "Like why Louise continues to be such a pain in the rear to you."

I opened my mouth to tell her not to bother; Louise wasn't going to listen to her anyway. But I shut it when I saw the determined look on Pat's face. Clearly, Louise wasn't the only one who wasn't going to listen to reason.

We headed across the restaurant toward Louise and Kat. They were both focused on eating and talking, so neither of them noticed us until we were right at their table.

"Good morning," I said. Both women looked up, startled, although Louise's expression almost immediately soured when she saw me. Kat was so surprised that she spilled her coffee on the table. "Fancy meeting both of you here. I didn't even realize you knew each other."

Louise shot me a brittle smile. "Good morning, Charlie. I'm surprised to see you here. I figured you had other ... plans."

"Oh, because you set me up with the cops?" I asked.

Louise patted her mouth with a napkin. "I don't know what you're talking about. All I did was my civic duty by telling the cops what I witnessed."

"Oh, give me a break," Pat said, rolling her eyes. "You couldn't wait to try and set up Charlie. What is wrong with you? Are you really so childish?"

Louise straightened up. "There's nothing childish about telling the cops that you saw the victim of a murder in a heated argument a few hours before he was killed."

"Oh for Pete's sake," Pat said, but I put a hand on her arm.

"You and I both know it wasn't a heated argument," I said. "And David was the one who was upset, not me. But that's not why I'm here." I turned to Kat. "I want to know why you lied to me about what happened to Abe."

Kat's eyes were round, a dumbfounded expression on her face. "Lied? I didn't lie to you. What are you talking about?"

"Kat wouldn't lie," Louise said, but her face was uncertain as she glanced at Kat.

"Oh, you two are best friends now?" I asked Louise before turning back to Kat. "You know exactly what I'm talking about."

Kat stared at me, a muscle twitching in her jaw. While lying might be a bit of an exaggeration, she definitely hadn't told me the full truth. Yes, David was obsessed with Ike, and probably seeing only what he wanted to see, but I didn't think he was so delusional as to have made something up out of whole cloth. I wasn't sure if I believed the "a witness saw Ike in the neighborhood" claim, as that would have surely made the cops more interested in Ike ... but I did believe something had triggered David and made him think that Ike was involved in Abe's death. And all that made me think Abe's death wasn't as cut and dry as Kat made it out to be.

It also made me wonder why Ike had left Sleepy Hollow in the first place. Would someone really quit his job and leave his home because of a single fight? Especially when it was clear Kat wasn't herself with everything that had happened to her.

Kat was hiding something, which would have been curious before David ended up dead and Ike ended up missing, but after? To paraphrase Shakespeare, something was definitely rotten in Denmark.

"Charlie, just stop it," Louise said. "Although I guess I shouldn't be surprised. Bullying someone to distract from your own guilt."

Kat was studying her half-eaten breakfast, her hair in her face again so I couldn't see her expression, but at that point, I had had enough with Louise. I whirled toward her, causing her to flinch slightly. "Oh, you want to talk about guilt? Great, let's have that conversation."

"So you're going to confess?" Louise asked, her voice full of bravado despite the uncertainty all over her face.

I ignored her barb. "What I want to know is how you knew David was going to be murdered."

Louise's mouth dropped open. "*What?*"

"You heard me. How did you know?"

"I have no idea what you're talking about." Louise was practically sputtering. "How dare you try and project your guilt on me!"

"If you didn't know, then why did you warn me about hanging out with David?"

"I didn't ... what are you talking about?"

"You told me to be careful about the friends I keep," I said. "Why would you warn me about spending time with David unless you knew he was going to be murdered?"

"I didn't ... that wasn't what I was doing." Louise's eyes were darting back and forth. She seemed to be trying to get Kat's attention, but Kat still had her gaze fixed firmly on her plate.

"Then what were you doing?"

"Maybe I was trying to do you a favor," Louise said. "Not that you deserve it."

My eyes widened. "A favor? How is that a favor? Unless you knew who David was."

"What does it matter who I knew or didn't know?" Louise asked. "I wasn't the one fighting with a murder victim."

"Everything okay here?" Sue had muscled her way in, giving us all a pointed look. "More coffee?" she asked, brandishing the pot.

"Sure," Louise said, pushing her cup toward her and giving Sue a smile that didn't reach her eyes. "Charlie and Pat were just going back to their table anyway. Weren't you?"

I flashed Louise a wide smile. "Yes. I think we're done here."

Chapter 16

After breakfast with Pat, I went home, fully intending on focusing on my tea business. I was running low on a couple of my most popular blends, not to mention all the paperwork I needed to catch up on. A lot of paperwork, actually. Ugh. That was the part I hated the most about the business, but as this was already turning into a crappy day, I figured it couldn't get much worse by spending it in my office.

Despite my intention to immediately head to work, I found myself in my kitchen brewing a pot of tea. I decided I deserved a break after the morning I'd had. Once the tea was done, I sat next to Midnight at the table, staring out the window at my garden covered with piles of dead leaves. There was an awful lot of them. I contemplated heading outside to rake them up and saving the paperwork for another day. Some manual labor would probably be therapeutic.

I had just finished my tea and was preparing to go tackle the leaves when the doorbell rang.

For a moment, I froze. I wasn't expecting anyone. Could it be Pat? Although she normally came right in, knocking as she did. Maybe it was a potential customer wanting to talk to me.

In my mind, I saw the grinning jack-o'-lantern sitting on my porch next to a Headless Horseman, just waiting for me to open the door and …

Stop it. I was being ridiculous. I needed to get my head on straight and fast. I couldn't allow myself to descend into fear, especially if I was truly being targeted by the police for a crime I didn't commit.

I brushed my hands on my jeans, straightened my shoulders, and headed over to the front door, determined to get back to my old self.

Despite that determination, I found myself pausing and needing to take a breath before peeking through the peephole.

I kept telling myself I was being silly—there was no need to steel myself for whoever (or whatever) was on my porch, yet I couldn't stop myself.

But nothing prepared me for who was there.

It was Kat.

It took a moment for my brain to process the information, as I had been so convinced it would either be the mundane (a customer) or something else completely.

The possibility of it being Kat had not even occurred to me.

I opened the door, and Kat's expression was immediately relieved. "Oh. I'm so glad you're home," she said, her words coming out in a rush. "I hope it's okay that I stopped by like this? Maybe I should have called first. I probably should have called and not just showed up."

"It's okay," I said, putting my hand out like I could physically stop the flow of words. "It's no problem. What do you need?"

She sucked in a breath. "Do you have a moment? I know it's a terrible imposition …"

"It's fine." I interrupted, stepping back. "Do you want to come in?"

She flashed me another relieved smile and stepped inside the house.

"Would you like some tea?" I asked, closing the door behind her.

"I'd love some," she said.

I gestured for her to follow me into the kitchen, where I got the hot water started for a fresh pot. I debated putting out cookies, but figured we had both just eaten breakfast.

I told her to have a seat while I finished with the tea. She perched gingerly on the edge of a chair, twisting a hunk of her hair with her finger. I was quiet, wanting to see if she would start talking, but she seemed to be waiting for me to join her at the table.

I placed the mug in front of her and sat down across from her. She thanked me but didn't touch it.

"So, what's up?" I asked, picking up my mug and blowing on it to cool it off.

Her hair was back in her face, so I couldn't tell if she was looking at me or not. "I wanted to talk about what you said this morning."

I nodded. "About you not telling me the truth?"

Her cheeks flushed. "It's not what it seems."

"Maybe you should explain."

She was silent for a moment. "This is about David, isn't it?" She lifted her head slightly, and some of her hair fell away from her face, allowing me to see her deep-brown eyes framed with thick lashes. It struck me how pretty she was. When I had first met her, she had seemed more waif-like, her beauty more insubstantial, like a fairy or an elf. But in that moment, her prettiness reminded me more of a cheerleader.

"What do you mean?"

"I mean, it's about what David said to you." Her eyes stared into mine. "Isn't it?"

There was an intensity about her that was a little disconcerting. I took a sip of tea, wanting a moment to get my thoughts in order. Of course Kat would assume David had said something to me. After all, she knew I had been talking to him. Everyone probably knew at this point, thanks to Louise.

But that still didn't mean I wanted to show my cards.

"He did mention an … alternative theory to what happened to Abe," I said.

Her cheeks turned a deeper red. She muttered something I couldn't hear before giving her head a quick shake. "Sorry," she said. "I shouldn't speak ill of the dead. But he just made me so mad."

"Why?"

"Why do you think?" She gestured wildly with her hand. "He's out spreading lies to people like you."

"So, Ike didn't have anything to do with Abe's death?"

"Of course not." Her tone was dismissive. "Abe's death was tragic, but Ike had nothing to do with it."

"Then why did David think he did?"

"I don't know. He had some history with Ike, or something." She picked up her mug but still didn't drink. "Not that it matters now."

I studied her. Her face was still flushed, and she still seemed upset. Was it anger? Fear? Or something else?

"Yes, but why Abe?" I persisted. "I'm sure there were other crimes in Sleepy Hollow. Why would David pick Abe's death to pin on Ike instead of some other crime?"

She looked at me like I was an idiot. "Because he knew Ike and I were together, that's why."

"But how did he know that?" I asked. "You told me that Ike was clear about nothing happening between you two until you had broken off your engagement to another man. How would David even know you were interested in each other?"

"Well …" she stuttered, her expression a little flummoxed. "He must have seen us together at some point."

"How?" I kept my tone soft and calm even as I continued to press. I wanted answers, and if she was going to appear at my doorstep, then I figured it was all fair game. "Were you two going places together? Even though you weren't together?"

"No. Not really," she amended. "We were together at school, of course. I'm guessing he must have seen us there."

"Did David work at the school, too?"

"No. He was some sort of journalist."

"Then how did David see you together, if he wasn't working at the school?"

"Probably because he was following Ike," she said, her voice agitated. "You have to understand, David was obsessed with Ike. He was convinced Ike was some … some psychopath. He was unhinged. Who knows what lengths David would go to in order to pin something on Ike?"

While what she said about David was true, there was something about Kat's defense that didn't sit quite right with me either. I decided to try a different tack. "I agree David was a little fixated on Ike, but is that the only thing going on?"

Kat's eyes narrowed slightly. "What do you mean?"

"Well …" I paused to take another sip of tea. "David implied there was more to the story of Abe's death. He seemed to suggest that maybe Ike was there that night."

"That's ridiculous," Kat said, but her face had gone pale underneath the red circles of her cheeks. "Ike was with me. I told you."

"David also said that you were saying what you needed to." I cocked my head. "Do you know what he meant by that?"

Kat stared at me as all the color slowly drained from her face. "You can't tell anyone," she begged.

"Can't tell anyone what?"

"What David told you!" She bit her lip and turned away from me. I waited for her to keep talking. "I didn't want anyone to know," she said.

"Know what?"

She still didn't answer, just kept chewing her bottom lip. Finally, she took a deep breath and turned to me. "David was blackmailing me."

"He was what?" I hadn't expected that.

"I didn't want to get into it," she said unhappily. "I mean, David is dead now, so it's done. And the last thing I want to do is ruin David's reputation. It's not like he's here to defend himself anymore. Nor can he hurt me anymore."

"I think you need to start from the beginning."

She sighed. "I wasn't speculating when I said David was monitoring the school. I don't know what tipped him off, but he somehow figured out how Ike and I felt about each other. I'm still not sure how. We were so careful, and it's not like we ever touched … well, anyway. David started showing up at school, pretending to be related to one of my students. I would see him during pick-ups and drop-offs, and even at one of our open houses. We chatted a few times, although thank goodness I never shared anything confidential about the child he was pretending to be related to. Then, one day I happened to see him at the grocery store. I was in the parking lot loading up my car when he walked by. I paused to say hi and ask him how he was doing. I didn't think anything of it, although I do remember he had a strange expression on his face. And that was when he told me who he really was."

"That must have been shocking," I said.

"You have no idea," Kat said. "At first, I was so horrified, all I wanted to do was get in my car and drive away. But I had a full cart of groceries I had to load. I told him to leave me alone, and if I saw him at the school I would call the cops, but it didn't seem to faze him. He told me the 'truth' about Ike, and that he had seen the way we looked at each other. He said it would be smart to stay away from him. It didn't matter what I said or how much I told him to leave me alone … he wouldn't stop talking.

"Finally, I got all my groceries into the car and was able to get away. I was shaking, I was so upset. Luckily, Abe wasn't home. I can't even imagine what would have happened. Anyway, as soon as I got the groceries into the house, I called Ike, who told me about his history with David." She paused to take a sip of tea, squeezing the mug between her hands.

"Is that when David started blackmailing you?" I asked. "Was he threatening to tell Abe about Ike?"

She shook her head. "No, the blackmail didn't start until after … after …" she swallowed hard and pushed her nearly untouched tea away. "Look, I didn't tell you the whole truth. Ike WAS there that night."

"He was?" Oh boy. Was THAT the evidence David had? That Ike had been there the night Abe was killed, and Kat lied about it? No wonder David was convinced that Ike had been guilty. I felt a slight pang that I had been so quick to not believe David while he was alive. Was it possible he had been the one telling the truth the whole time, and Ike really was the psychopath?

Kat nodded miserably. "It's all my fault," she said. "When I got home and saw Abe lying there in a pool of blood ... I just panicked. I probably should have called the cops, but instead, I called Ike. He told me to call the cops and he would be right over, but I was so hysterical, I couldn't think straight. I just ... I kept pacing the house, over and over, replaying in my mind what I had done and wondering if it was my fault. Ike arrived, and I still hadn't called the cops. He calmed me down, but by then, so much time had elapsed, and Ike thought him being there as the 'other' man would bring too much attention to him ... that the cops would assume he had something to do with the murder, since Abe would be considered his rival. So, I called the cops, and Ike slipped away."

"And you told the cops you were alone," I said.

Kat bowed her head, her misery reflected in the set of her body.

Of course. It was so obvious now. Someone, maybe even David himself, must have seen Ike that night. And when Kat denied Ike being there at all, of course David would assume the worst.

I sighed. "So, when did the blackmail start?"

"A couple of days later. I was still at home, trying to deal with, well, with everything. David came to the house and told me he knew I was lying."

"So, what did he want? Money?"

She lifted her head to look at me. "No. He wanted me to tell the truth and send Ike, the love of my life, to prison. I refused, of course. But he said if I didn't tell, then he would.

"So, I tried a different tack. I told him how Abe abused me and how much I needed Ike. That without Ike, I wouldn't be able to live."

She paused and swallowed hard. "I think ... I think ..." Her voice dropped to a whisper, even though we were alone in my home and only Midnight was there to overhear her. "I think he took that to mean that Ike was abusing me, too, and even though I was away from Abe, I needed some time to get away from Ike."

I stared at her, uncomprehendingly. "I'm sorry. Are you saying you let David think that Ike was abusing you?"

Kat's eyes widened. "No, it wasn't like that. It's … it's hard to explain." She bit her lip again, and I could see a couple drops of blood forming. "I didn't realize that was what he was thinking until it was too late. He was already convinced of Ike's guilt. I knew there wouldn't be any way to change his mind. David already had a terrible opinion of Ike, so I just … I just used it." She shrugged slightly.

I was still staring at her. "What do you mean, you 'used' it?"

She lifted a hand and began to twist a lock of hair again. "It sounds so terrible when you say it like that. It wasn't like I was using it for my own gain, but for Ike's. I figured the longer I could string David along, the colder the case would get, and the less interest the cops would have in interviewing Ike. Plus, there was always the chance the real killers would be found. So, I just thought I would … wait him out."

I was having a lot of trouble wrapping my head around what Kat had done to someone she claimed was the love of her life. "But you let David think Ike was an abuser."

"Only to protect Ike," she said, a note of desperation in her voice.

"But still …" I shook my head. "Did Ike know?"

She was silent.

And that's when the pieces all clicked into place. "Is THAT the real reason Ike left? Because he found out you let David think he's an abuser?"

"Now you sound like Ike," she said with a tinge of exasperation. "It wasn't LIKE that. I keep saying it, and no one is listening to me! I never would have let anyone think Ike was like Abe. I wouldn't have let it go that far. It was only David, and no one believed him anyway. Everyone knew he couldn't see straight when it came to Ike. So, it didn't matter what David thought or didn't think. All that mattered was keeping Ike out of jail."

"Yes, but ..." I said, my mind sorting out the original conversation I had with David. "David ended up saying something to the police, didn't he?"

She had the grace to look embarrassed. "I didn't think he would. I swear. I thought he trusted me. But yes. He did go to the police. I denied it all, of course, when the cops questioned me."

At least now it all made sense: why Ike quit his job and left so suddenly (he also probably thought the book deal was a gift from God) and why Kat was desperate to find him and explain. It also explained David's cryptic remark about Kat having said what she needed to. If David truly thought Ike was abusing her, he would also have assumed that Kat was lying for her own safety. "So, Ike left and ..."

"Well, David left next, trying to track down Ike," she said. "David was really upset about the cops not taking him seriously. He was bound and determined to get the proof he needed."

"What about whoever saw Ike that night?" I asked. "I'm assuming someone in the neighborhood saw him leave. Or was it David himself?" That would be something, if David was the one who had seen Ike leaving the neighborhood. Unless David lived near Kat, it would certainly make him look more unstable and stalker-ish than he already did.

Kat waved her hand dismissively. "It doesn't matter who it was. The cops didn't take it seriously, so clearly, it wasn't an issue."

"I suppose you're right," I said, even though to me the case was getting more and more puzzling. If Ike was there that night, and David knew there was a witness, then why wouldn't the cops have taken it seriously? But I could see Kat was done with that conversation, so I decided to move on. "So, first Ike left, and then David decided to follow him to try and get this so-called 'proof.'" Now, it also made more sense why David wanted me to record whatever story Ike told me. If Ike was lying to the cops, it was possible whatever he told me would be different enough from what he told the cops that the cops would decide to re-open the case. It still seemed more like a Hail Mary, but at least I could understand David's reasoning more.

Kat bobbed her head. "Yes. So I, of course, also had to follow. Not just because I wanted to beg Ike's forgiveness and convince him to take me back, but to also warn him that David was following him, and to be careful."

"Do you know where Ike is?"

Kat's face fell. "No. I haven't seen him since Sleepy Hollow. I was really hoping I had finally gotten lucky here, when I found out he was staying at the Redemption Inn. But no one has seen him in days. His stuff is still here, but where is he?" She clenched both hands into tight fists, and for a moment, I was worried she might start pounding the table in frustration.

"Good question," I said. "I think a lot of people would like to know what happened to Ike."

She jolted at the sound of my voice, almost like she had forgotten I was there. I could see her chest heave as she took several deep breaths and tucked her hands under the table. "Anyway, thank you for taking the time to talk to me, especially since I just stopped by unannounced. I'm sure you have things you need to be doing." She smiled at me as she stood up, but it seemed perfunctory.

"No problem," I said, also rising to my feet. "I'm glad you came by."

"Well, I can see why you were confused," she said. "It's unfortunate that David found Ike, as well."

I cocked my head. "David found Ike? I didn't realize that. David made it seem like he hadn't seen Ike in Redemption, either."

"Well ... I mean that he found out Ike was here," Kat said. She was visibly flustered. "I don't know if he actually saw Ike or not. I just know he found out that Ike had a hotel room booked and that he tracked you down."

"I see," I said, continuing to study her. Her face and neck were flushed. "Do you think David had anything to do with Ike's disappearance?" Even though I didn't think David had seen Ike in Redemption either, Kat's reaction had piqued my interest, and I wanted to hear her thoughts.

Kat's eyes widened. "You think David might have done something to Ike?" She pressed a hand against her chest.

"I have no idea," I said. "But it's possible, don't you think? David's focus on Ike is unhealthy, to say the least. So would it be that much of a stretch to think he might be responsible for Ike's disappearance?"

Kat's fingers clutched at her shirt as her eyes grew more round. "You think ... you think something happened to Ike?" Her voice dropped to a whisper. "Like, you think he's ...." She swallowed hard, unable to finish the sentence. All the color drained from her face, and she started to sway.

"Hey," I said quickly, reaching out to steady her. "Maybe we should sit down for a moment."

Kat started violently shaking her head. "No. No, I have to go. Right now."

"I don't think you should be going anywhere, at least until you've had a moment to collect yourself," I said.

"I'm fine," she said, pushing my hand away. "I just ... I have to go. If something happened to Ike ..."

"Kat, we don't know if anything happened to Ike," I said gently. "All we know for sure is that he hasn't been back to his hotel room. There could be a lot of reasons for that, though, and it doesn't mean he was ... hurt." I almost said "killed," but thought maybe I should soften it, as she still didn't look well.

It apparently was a good thing I did, as she visibly winced at "hurt." "I need to look for him," she said. "It's not like Ike to just disappear like this. Maybe something did happen to him, and now it's been days and ..." she swallowed hard again. "Thank you for everything, but I need to go."

I wanted to protest again, as her color still didn't look right, but she was already pushing past me and heading to the front door. "Just be careful," I said. "Drive safely. And if you need a moment, don't be afraid to pull over and just sit for a few minutes."

"I'll be fine," she said again, not turning around as she reached the front door and let herself out.

I watched her go, her shoulders hunched over as she hurried to her car, and hoped she was right.

I also wondered what else she was hiding.

Chapter 17

After Kat left, I cleaned up the kitchen, which didn't take long. Mainly, I had to wash her barely touched mug. I idly wondered if she didn't generally drink tea or if she just didn't like mine. Not that it mattered—it wouldn't have hurt my feelings if she had declined.

I filed it away as another puzzling fact about Kat.

Afterward, I put my coat on and went out to rake the yard. The paperwork could wait another day. My mind was spinning around too much to focus, and raking the leaves would keep my body occupied while my mind pondered.

It was a beautiful fall day. The sun was shining, but it was still cool with a slight nip. The air held that fall scent of decaying and dead plants and leaves. I quickly decided I had made the right decision. It had been a while since I'd done any yardwork, and I realized how much my body missed it. I told myself I needed a regular exercise routine, at least in the winter. In the summer, gardening kept me fairly active, but once it got cold, I became much more sedentary, and I did miss moving around.

"There you are."

I jumped and turned. Wyle was standing near my outdoor table and chairs. I had been so engrossed in my raking, I hadn't even heard him approach. "You scared me."

A faint smile touched his lips. "I didn't mean to, but I'm not surprised. That's some pretty mean raking you were doing. What did those poor leaves ever do to you?"

I looked down at the mounds I had been creating. They did look a bit ragged around the edges. "They scattered themselves all over the yard. Next time, they should fall into neat piles. Then, we won't have this issue."

Wyle's smile widened. "Hopefully, they learned their lesson. Do you have a moment, or should I come back later?"

I didn't answer right away. Instead, I set the rake on the ground next to me and leaned against it. I still wasn't sure how I felt about what had happened that morning. I knew Wyle was just doing his job, and yet ... how could he really think I had anything to do with David's death? I understood that he needed to ask me those questions, especially since Louise likely raised a stink about my conversation with David, but did he have to make it so official?

I wanted to give him a snarky reply, but I bit it back, and instead answered more honestly. "I don't know if I have a moment," I said. "After what happened earlier, I don't know if I can trust you."

He stared at me, his expression unreadable. "Fair enough. But I'd like to explain. Will you let me?"

Even if I wanted to, I couldn't say no to that. I picked up my rake and walked over to him, feeling a pleasant tiredness in my arms. Definitely another sign I had probably been at it for long enough. "Let's go inside. I don't know about you, but I could use a cup of tea."

"That would hit the spot," Wyle said, following me. I leaned my rake against the house, intending to put it away later, along with collecting all the leaves I had piled up.

Once in the kitchen, I removed my coat, but before I could hang it by the front door, Wyle took it and did it for me. It was oddly chivalrous and comforting, like we were a couple who knew each other's habits. Almost immediately, I pushed that thought out of my head. That was the last thing I needed to be thinking. Instead, I bustled around the kitchen, starting the tea and laying out some cookies on a plate. After all that raking, I felt like I could use a treat.

Wyle waited until I had put everything on the table and sat down across from him before he started to talk. "I didn't have much choice about this morning," he said.

I picked up my tea but didn't drink it. "Is that your way of apologizing?"

He gave me a sideways smile. "Sort of. I don't know." He picked up a cookie but didn't eat it, breaking it into pieces instead. "Look, we did everything by the book. We had credible witnesses say you had an argument with the victim a few hours before his death. Of course we needed to question you. It would have been a miscarriage of justice if we didn't ask you about it."

"I don't have a problem with you having to ask me questions," I said. "It's the way it was all done. Bringing me in like a suspect. Heck, someone even leaked to the press that I was wanted for questioning."

"No one knew it was you," Wyle said quickly. "Your name wasn't in there."

"Louise knew," I said, darkly. "There was enough detail for her to figure it out. And you know how this town is with gossip. Everyone would know. Why would you leak that?"

Wyle sighed heavily. "I didn't. And before you ask, I don't officially know who did."

My gaze sharpened. "Officially?" Pat's warning from earlier, that all wasn't what it seemed in the Redemption Police Department, came flooding back.

Wyle's mouth flattened. "Just leave it. For now."

I studied him, but he had his cop face back on, and I couldn't read it. "Wyle, what's going on?" I asked.

"You know what's going on. We're in the middle of a murder investigation ..."

I shook my head. "No. There's something else happening here. Something you aren't telling me. Is there someone in the police department trying to railroad me or pin this on me somehow?"

"You're not being set up," Wyle started.

I gave him a hard look. "But ..."

He sighed and rubbed his face, looking more exhausted than normal. "Charlie, you're going to have to trust me," he said. "You have to know I have your back. Even if it doesn't look like it."

Pat's voice floated through my head. *You'd be surprised.* I shivered. "I do trust you, but you're kind of scaring me."

"As soon as I can, I'll tell you what's going on, but right now …" He picked up his tea but didn't drink. "Right now, I have to keep my cards close to my chest. Understand?"

I picked up my tea as well, craving the warmth. It sounded to me like Wyle was doing a little investigation of his own, maybe inside the police department. I started to get a little worried for him. "Understood. But what does that mean for David's murder investigation? Do I need a lawyer?"

"I don't think so. At least not yet," Wyle said. I shivered again, despite myself. Wyle saw it and frowned slightly. "I promise I'll tell you if you do need one, but for right now, you don't. I know I'm not telling you anything you don't already know when I say that Louise did talk to us, but it wasn't just her. Other people in that lobby also witnessed how heated your conversation was with David. But as you pointed out, there are also multiple witnesses who saw you and David leave separately, and there's no evidence that you returned. So, for now, it's a dead end."

For now. While I suspected Wyle thought he was being reassuring, I wasn't feeling very reassured. "So, what should I do?"

"What I'm always telling you. Stay out of the investigation. Let the professionals handle it."

"But the professionals seem like the ones out to get me."

Wyle exhaled hard through his nose. "There's no evidence to suggest anyone is specifically out to get you," he said. "That said, you do need to be careful. I'm not sure what's going on, and until I have a better handle on it, it would be better if you just stayed out of things."

"Fine," I said. While the thought of sitting at home twiddling my thumbs while Louise and who knows who else ran around whispering lies and ruining my reputation infuriated me, I could also see Wyle's point.

Wyle put his mug down and stood up. "I promise I'll keep you informed, okay? We'll get to the bottom of this."

"I appreciate that," I said, not moving. "Does that mean you don't want to hear about Kat coming to visit me?"

He stared at me before sitting back down and pulling out his notebook. "Start from the beginning, please."

I told him everything that happened, from seeing Louise and Kat in Aunt May's to the strange conversation with Kat at my house. He didn't say much, mostly just scribbled notes as fast as he could.

"Were you able to get in touch with the Sleepy Hollow Police Department?" I asked when I had finished my recap.

He shook his head, still peering at his notes. "But you can be sure I'm going to make it a priority. Along with finding Ike."

"I'm starting to wonder if Ike is even still in Redemption," I said. "This town isn't that big. How many places could he actually hide in?"

Wyle glanced up from nis notebook. "You think he left?"

"Maybe. Although I don't know why he wouldn't have checked out if he was moving to the next place."

"Maybe he didn't want anyone to know he left."

I felt that chill again. "Like so he could use it as an alibi?"

Wyle's mouth was a flat line. "Exactly."

A part of me wanted to defend Ike. I still couldn't believe that Ike was a killer. But Pat's words about my using Ike as a wedge between Wyle and me floated through my head, and I forced myself to pause, take a deep breath, and try a different tack. "So, in other words, you think Ike killed David, but no one suspects him, because he's been missing?"

Wyle looked at me. "You don't think that's possible?"

"It's just … that seems really cold-blooded," I said. "Plus, Ike was missing at least a couple of days before David was killed. You think he was planning that far in advance?"

"If David was trying to ruin Ike's life, which it sounds like he was, why wouldn't he?" Wyle asked. "For all we know, Ike has been planning this for months, since David chased him out of Sleepy Hollow. He was just waiting for the perfect opportunity."

"I suppose that makes sense," I said, but I couldn't reconcile the picture of Ike in my head with him being that ruthless.

Wyle noticed a change in my tone and shot me a look. "What do you think happened to him? The Headless Horseman got him?"

"Well, the thought crossed my mind. Ike did think he was being haunted, and the Headless Horseman does like to make his victims disappear." I paused as I played with my mug. "No, I was actually thinking something less … supernatural."

Wyle's gaze was sharp. "Like he was murdered."

Having Wyle say it like that, out loud, made it more real somehow … like he had somehow spoken it into existence. "Something like that."

"It's possible," Wyle said. "And it's definitely a possibility we've been looking into. But so far, we haven't come across any evidence of that."

"Well, that's good, I guess."

Wyle glanced at the clock, winced, and tucked his notebook back into his pocket. "Now I definitely need to go, but keep me posted if anything else comes up."

"I will," I said, standing up with him. "I appreciate all you're doing."

He studied me, and something seemed to pass between us—something unspoken, with its own energy. I sensed Wyle could feel it, too, but we also both knew it wasn't the time or place. "I'll let you know if there are any new developments," he finally said.

"Thank you. I appreciate that."

Wyle flashed me a crooked smile before making his way out of the kitchen and to the front door, leaving me alone with my unwelcome and uncomfortable thoughts.

* * *

After I cleaned up the kitchen, I headed back outside to finish up the yard. I did a lot of composting, adding most of the leaves to that pile. It shouldn't have taken as long as it did, but more than once, I found myself pausing and searching the yard, sure there was someone there, watching me. I could feel eyes on the back of my neck so strong, it was like they were burning a hole through my skin. But no matter how hard I searched, I saw nothing but birds and squirrels.

My imagination was clearly running wild. I finished the job as quickly as I could before going back into the house to start dinner.

I tried to focus on the tasks in front of me instead of on my swirling, worried thoughts. I wished I could call Pat and talk things through, but she had prior plans with her adult daughter.

I was in the middle of chopping an onion when the doorbell rang. I froze, knife in the air. Normally, I didn't think twice when the doorbell rang. It wasn't uncommon for customers to stop by without calling first, as everyone knew I worked out of my house.

But now, with all the bizarre happenings, I wasn't sure what to think.

As I stood there, the bell rang again, the normally cheerful chimes echoing through the house like a blaring warning. I placed the knife down on the chopping board, wiped my hands off, and headed for the door. I at least needed to see who it was, even if I chose not to answer it.

Just in case, I avoided the floorboards that squeaked and peered through the peephole. A man was standing there. He had thick glasses, short brown hair, and the thin, flabby build of someone who never worked out yet was still able to maintain his weight.

I recognized him immediately, cursing under my breath. Tad from *The Redemption Times*. The last person I wanted to see.

I had no intention of talking to him.

I whirled away from the door to head back to the kitchen when the bell rang again. Even though a part of me knew I should just walk away and ignore him, another part of me was exhausted and fed up. "Go away, Tad," I yelled. "I'm not giving you a quote."

His voice was muffled on the other side of the door. "So, you want me to say you refuse to comment?"

"I'm not playing this game with you," I shouted back.

"The public has a right to know."

"I'm not running for Congress. I'm a private citizen, and I have a right to my privacy."

"There's been a terrible murder, and you're a suspect," Tad said. "You don't have any privacy rights."

His words were like knives stabbing me in the gut, but I refused to let him see how rattled they made me. "Oh, just go away," I said, infusing my voice with as much disdain as I could. "I haven't been accused or convicted of any crime, so my privacy rights are perfectly intact."

"Come on, Charlie." The voice was wheedling. "I just have a few questions. Don't you want to share your side of the story?"

"Goodbye, Tad," I said and made a point of walking away. Behind me, I heard more shouting and banging on the door, along with more doorbell ringing.

I wondered if I should go back and tell him I was calling the cops, as he was on private property, but decided I'd give him a few more minutes to realize I wasn't coming out. It took a little longer than I would have preferred, but eventually, the noise died down.

As soon as it did, I sank down at the kitchen table, my appetite gone. If Tad was here, that could only mean things were going from bad to worse with the investigation.

Was it possible I was going to be arrested?

I eyed the phone, but it was silent. Wyle promised he'd call me if something changed. Should I call him? Or would that cause more problems?

Man, I wished Pat was around.

After wrestling with myself for a bit, I finally got up and forced myself to finish making dinner. I had been working on a beef stew with mashed potatoes on the off chance of Wyle coming by to give me an update. It would be an easy meal to keep warm, and I could quickly heat up the leftovers in a pinch.

Now, with what Tad had said to me, it seemed even more vital to have a meal prepared.

But Wyle didn't come by. I hovered in the kitchen waiting for the phone to ring or a knock at the door, but neither happened. Instead, I drank way too much tea and finally forced myself to eat a small portion of the stew and potatoes.

I stayed up until nearly midnight, even though I was exhausted and wired, but I didn't want to be in bed in case Wyle had been working late and decided to stop by. Finally, I decided he wasn't coming short of an emergency.

Reluctantly, I headed up to bed. Tomorrow would be soon enough to decide my next step.

Chapter 18

The sound of a horse galloping jolted me out of a fitful sleep. I didn't think. I just acted.

I threw back the covers, grabbed a robe that I had tossed over one of the chairs, and ran out of my bedroom. It probably wasn't smart, but the anger was building inside of me.

I was exhausted and sick of it. I'd had enough. I was done.

I was going to get to the bottom of what was going on, so I could move on with my life.

My first stop was my office, where I snatched up the baseball bat that I had left propped up in the corner along with a flashlight. I had another flashlight in the living room, but this one was heavier, with a nice strong beam. Plus, it had some heft to it, so if for some reason I lost my baseball bat, I could use it in the same manner.

Weapons in hand, I ran down the stairs and straight to the front door. Before the voice of reason in my head could talk me out of such an impulsive move, I flung it open and charged down the porch, waving my flashlight around as I brandished my baseball bat.

Almost immediately, the sound of the horse galloping disappeared, like it was simply switched off. Which made me think maybe it WAS switched off.

Like it had been kids all along, playing a recording of a horse galloping in the middle of the night.

The idea that a bunch of kids playing a prank had caused this entire series of events to unravel, culminating in the death of a man, made me even more furious.

"Who's there?" I shouted, shaking my flashlight. "Come out and show yourself!"

Silence.

"Whoever you are, I know you're not a ghost. Or the Headless Horseman," I said. "The police WILL figure out who you are, so you might as well come clean now."

Still no response. I paused in the middle of the driveway, slowly moving the flashlight beam around while looking for anything out of place at all. But as far as I could tell, there was nothing other than the normal trees and bushes that surrounded my home. I even attempted to search my neighbor's cornfields, but the flashlight beam didn't reach far enough.

From down the street, I heard the sound of a car start, and I automatically swung my flashlight toward it. Of course I didn't see anything, but I wondered who would be starting their car in the middle of the night. I lived in a fairly quiet residential neighborhood. Most of the people were tucked up inside their homes at that time of night.

Was it the kids behind the prank? My gut said yes, but, of course, I had no proof. I was way too far away from the car to see anything. I didn't even have anything suspicious I could point to, like footsteps running away.

Ugh. I stood there frozen, wondering what to do next.

Even though I was sure whoever was behind the pranks was gone, I continued searching the area with my eyes. But of course, I didn't find anything. It was too dark, even with the bright beam of my flashlight. I needed to wait until the sun came out.

Now that the danger seemed to have passed and my breathing and heart rate were slowing down, I was becoming aware of how cold it was outside. It was October, and the air had a bite to it that promised winter wasn't far behind. The driveway was icy under my bare feet, as I hadn't wanted to take the time to put shoes on.

This was nuts. I needed to go back inside where it was warm, especially since there wasn't anything I could do anyway. I hurried back in, locking the door behind me and immediately going to the kitchen to make some tea.

Midnight was up, as well, and waiting for me on the stairs. He probably sensed that despite how exhausted I was, sleep was done for the night.

Luckily, I only had a few hours to wait until sunrise.

* * *

As soon as it was light enough, I was back outside, this time appropriately dressed in jeans, a sweatshirt, a jacket, and shoes. I walked up and down my cul-de-sac street, searching behind trees and bushes, but there was nothing that seemed out of place. All I found were a few broken branches and some indents in the ground that could have been footprints, which could of course been from anyone. It wasn't unusual for my neighbors to walk their dogs past my house or for the neighborhood kids to play in the woods there.

There was no way for me to prove it had anything to do with my late-night visitors.

I kept going, walking up the street to where I thought I'd heard the car drive off, but of course, there was nothing there. What was I expecting? An oil puddle? A cigarette butt? A note with the words "The prankster was here"?

Like that would prove anything.

Frustrated, I headed back to my house. It was a beautiful morning, the air crisp and cool, smelling of dried leaves and wood smoke. My footsteps padding along on the asphalt was the only sound I could hear. On the surface, I appeared to be completely alone, yet I didn't feel alone.

Again, I felt like I was being watched.

Even though I told myself I was likely on edge from everything that had been happening, I still found myself speeding up my steps. The sooner I got home, the better I would feel.

I had almost made it when the newspaper boy whizzed by on his dirt bike, swerving around me to toss the paper in my driveway.

"Thanks," I called out with a wave.

He didn't acknowledge me, which was a little unusual. Whenever I was up early enough to see him, he always waved back. But he was also a teenager, and teenagers were moody.

I figured I probably shouldn't take it personally.

Still, it made me uneasy. Especially as I kept seeing Tad pounding on my door in my mind's eye. *There's been a terrible murder, and you're a suspect.*

I found myself hurrying to collect the paper and head into the house. My hands were trembling as I slid off the rubber band and started to unroll it.

The headline blared at me at the same time my phone started ringing.

Redemption's Own Arsenic and Old Lace? Local Tea Maker Questioned in the Murder of Visiting Journalist.

My heart sank. Oh no.

The phone ringing cut through the fog in my head, and I answered it without thinking.

"Did you see the paper?" Pat's voice barked through the phone. I found my eyes flicking toward the clock. Pat was always an early riser, but this seemed particularly early even for her.

"I'm holding it in my hands."

"I'll be right over." The phone went dead.

I replaced the receiver and automatically went to make tea, my movements wooden. What on Earth was I going to do? I wondered if I should call Wyle or wait for him to call me. And why *hadn't* he called yet? Why was it taking him so long to reach out?

Or maybe I should be finding a lawyer, I thought. Thank goodness Pat was on her way over. I needed someone with a clear head to help me figure out what my next steps should be.

There was a knock at the door, which startled me so much, I almost dropped the mug I was taking down from the cupboard. Pat couldn't have arrived that fast. Could she?

Hesitantly, I headed toward the front door, peering through the peephole, my whole body tense.

But there was no one there.

I frowned as I kept looking. Had I imagined the knock? No, I was sure I hadn't.

So, where did whoever it was go?

Unless … was my prankster back? Did whoever it was leave a jack -o'-lantern on my porch—one they had planned to leave the night before, until I came storming out of my house, so they instead came back this morning?

A flare of anger rushed through me again, and I flung the door open, ready to charge out and confront the prankster.

Instead, I found nothing. No sign of a person or a jack-o'-lantern.

I rubbed my forehead. Maybe I did imagine the knock after all. It wouldn't be that surprising, with all the stress I'd been under.

I turned to go back into the house when a flash of white caught my eye. A folded piece of paper was tucked under the green-and-gold welcome mat.

The bile rose in my throat as I bent to pick it up. I was sure it wasn't there earlier.

I stepped out onto the porch and glanced around. As far as I could see, there was nothing there. But I was sure someone was watching me. I could feel their eyes crawling all over me.

I swallowed hard, remembering how I was sure someone had been out there as I searched my neighborhood, too. Was whoever left this note already in place, watching me?

Suddenly, I couldn't stand being outside. I felt way too exposed. I turned and went back into the house, firmly closing and locking the door behind me. I took a deep breath, forced myself to relax, and examined the piece of paper.

It appeared to be plain white typewriter paper folded in half. Carefully, and with a certain amount of trepidation, I unfolded it.

I'm sorry.

The two words were handwritten in black, ballpoint ink. There was nothing else.

I was even more puzzled than before. Who would leave me an anonymous apology? I wasn't sure what I expected—probably something more like a threat or maybe a cryptic clue—but "I'm sorry"?

I was still staring at the note when the sound of a quick, sharp knock followed by the turning of the knob startled me, making me jump.

More knocking. "Charlie? You there?"

It was Pat. I normally left the door unlocked when I knew she was coming over—not that it mattered, as she had her own key. I returned to let her in. "Sorry," I said.

Pat came in, her face concerned. In her arms was an excited Tiki, dressed in pink. Pat put her on the ground, and she made a beeline toward me to give me a welcome kiss. "It's fine. I totally understand why you're being safe," Pat said.

"It's not that," I replied, handing her the note.

Her brow wrinkled as she read it. "I'm sorry?"

"We better go in the kitchen," I said. "I have a lot to tell you."

Over tea and pumpkin muffins I had made in honor of Halloween, I shared with her everything that had happened, starting from when Kat had arrived unexpectedly and ending with the note left that morning.

"My goodness," Pat said when I was done. Tiki was on her lap, and Pat absentmindedly fed her a homemade pumpkin dog biscuit. "I'm going to have to think twice before making any plans the next time you're suspected of murder."

"Things do move fast around here," I agreed.

"I don't even know where to start," Pat fretted as she picked up a muffin.

"I know. What do you know about corruption in the Redemption Police Department?"

"'Corruption' is probably too strong of a word," Pat said. "It's more like ... concerns about irregularities."

"Irregularities?"

"Let me put it another way," Pat said. "Before you arrived and discovered your knack for solving crimes, most of the strange disappearances and whatnot were never solved. And when people asked, there was never a good response ... it was always, 'That's just what happens in Redemption.' Sadly, most people, including myself, more or less accepted that explanation. We all live here, so we get that a lot of weird, unexplained things happen. But then you arrived, along with Wyle, and suddenly, cases were getting solved. And that has brought up more questions about why Redemption's Finest couldn't do the same before you."

"Maybe the cases weren't solvable," I said.

Pat didn't look convinced. "Maybe. But I suspect there's something else going on. Whether it's laziness, or a lack of talent, or corruption. I tend to think it's not the latter, but regardless, I have no doubt that there are those in the police department who would like nothing more than to see you go down for murder."

I swallowed hard, feeling a chill run down my spine. "What about Murphy? He wasn't solving cases, either." When I had first moved to Redemption, I had a couple of run-ins with Murphy, mostly due to the disappearances that had happened shortly after I arrived, including Louise's brother Jesse. I knew Murphy thought I was more involved than I had let on, but seeing as he couldn't prove anything and Louise's accusations didn't count, he ended up dropping it.

"I don't know about Murphy," Pat said. "I always thought he was one of the good guys in the department, but as you mentioned, there were a lot of cases he wasn't able to solve, either. He might be the most embarrassed one there. He's been in that department forever and has a ton of experience. You and Wyle showing up and getting cases solved left and right ..." she held up both hands in question.

It had never occurred to me that my solving cases would somehow be embarrassing for the Redemption Police Department, but with Pat's explanation, it made a lot of sense.

"Well, if they really are embarrassed, and they think that's going to somehow stop me, they have another thing coming," I said. "Especially since they're now pointing the finger at me."

"No kidding," Pat said. "So, what's the plan? Figure out who is sending you apology notes? Dig into what really happened to Abe in Sleepy Hollow? Something else?"

"Hopefully, Wyle is calling the Sleepy Hollow Police Department," I said.

Pat's face darkened. "Speaking of Wyle, where is he? Has he been in touch about this?" She rattled the newspaper.

"Not yet. I can't decide if I should reach out first or wait."

Pat's mouth flattened. "As much as I'd like to tell you to track him down, you probably need to wait. If there really is something off in that department, you showing up to talk to Wyle will probably cause even more problems."

"Probably," I sighed, breaking off a piece of the pumpkin muffin. "Hey … do you think that apology note could be from someone in the police department who is trying to set me up?"

Pat snorted. "I was thinking it was from Tad, who knows he's being a jerk."

"Tad? No way. Louise would be more likely to apologize than Tad."

"Speaking of Louise, I'd like to know how much she had to do with this." Pat rattled the newspaper again.

I frowned. "You think Louise might have been the one talking to Tad?"

"I think it's more likely than the Redemption Police Department," Pat said. "Look, I know on the surface that this article looks bad. But what is it really saying? That you were questioned because you were seen talking to David. That's it. There's nothing in here that could be construed as being an official quote from the police. This whole thing screams that it's someone outside of the department leaking it."

"But Louise wouldn't know anything," I said. "And you just said some of the officers might resent me. Are you sure they wouldn't use this opportunity to paint a negative picture of me?"

Pat opened her mouth to answer, but before she could, the doorbell rang. "That better be Wyle," she said, getting to her feet. "I'll get the door. If it is him, we'll need more tea."

"Or coffee," I said, standing. My eyes were gritty from lack of sleep, and I thought I could use a cup myself.

Pat's face perked up. "Coffee sounds like a fabulous idea. As much as I love your tea, today feels like it's going to require caffeine."

"My thought exactly," I said as Pat went to the door, Tiki on her heels.

It was Wyle. I could hear Pat's voice as she lectured him. "How could you let this happen?"

Wyle's voice was grim. "Trust me, I want to figure that out as much as you do."

He appeared in the kitchen holding Tiki, who was busy giving him welcome kisses. Pat was standing behind him, her hands on her hips. "I hope you have more to share than you're 'looking into it.'"

"Morning, Wyle. Tea or coffee?" I asked.

Wyle's face was relieved. "Coffee."

"It should be ready in a minute," I said, getting out the mugs and cream. "So, are you here to tell me I need to get a lawyer?"

"Unless you're planning to sue the Redemption paper for libel, I would say no."

Pat's eyes widened. "Libel? Is the paper lying?"

"They're sure getting close to the line," Wyle said, sitting down at the table as I brought the coffee over. "No one seriously suspects you of killing David."

"What about unseriously? Anyone like that around?" I asked as I took my seat at the table, passing a mug of coffee over to Pat. I was only half-joking. While I suspected that Wyle was trying to ease my mind, I still couldn't shake the thought that he wasn't telling me the whole story.

He threw me a look over his mug. "You're not going to be arrested."

He still wasn't answering my question, but I decided to leave it. At least for the moment. I still had a lot of unanswered questions to focus on. "Then where is this coming from?"

Wyle's mouth was pressed into a thin line. "I'd like to know that myself."

"So you don't think it was from the police department?" Pat asked.

He shook his head. "No one is leaking information to the paper. I can pretty much guarantee it."

Pat looked at me. "I told you. It WAS Louise."

Wyle glanced at her. "Do you have any proof of that?"

"Other than the fact that everyone knows she's been trying to get rid of Charlie for years?" Pat retorted.

Wyle's lips twitched into a faint smile. "She was already on my list to question. Anyone else I should add?"

"Claire," I said.

Pat looked at me in surprise. "You think *Claire* was the leak?"

"Of course not," I said. "But she and Louise were at that same meeting. I'm wondering if Claire noticed anything suspicious."

Wyle's face was thoughtful as he jotted down her name. "We already asked her if she had witnessed the argument between you and David. But a follow-up wouldn't be a bad idea."

"What did she say about the argument?" I asked.

"That she hadn't witnessed anything, but she did corroborate when you left," Wyle said.

"Well, that's something," I said.

"The more people who back up your story, the better," Pat agreed.

"Is that it? Anyone else?" Wyle asked.

"What about the Sleepy Hollow angle?" I asked. "Did you find out anything more about Abe's death?"

"Actually, yes," Wyle said, flipping back through his notebook while simultaneously reaching for a muffin. "I was able to finally reach the lead detective."

"What did he say?"

Wyle broke off a piece of muffin and popped it into his mouth. "It was much like what Kat had said. On the night of April 18, Kat returned home to find Abe dead in his kitchen and the home ransacked. She called the cops, and when they arrived, they found her in the kitchen. She was hysterical."

"How did he die?" I asked.

"He had been stabbed with one of the kitchen knives," Wyle said. "He had also been hit in the head with a frying pan. The cops determined that Abe had come home, found the robbery in progress, and tried to intervene. The robber or robbers panicked, first hitting him on the head with the pan and then stabbing him."

"That seems like overkill," Pat said.

"Hence why the cops thought the robber had panicked and overreacted," Wyle said.

"Any evidence it was someone Abe knew?" I asked.

Wyle raised an eyebrow. "Like Ike? Detective Arnold didn't think so. There had been a slew of burglaries in that neighborhood over the past few months, so it fit the MO—someone breaking into an empty house, trashing it, and stealing small items like jewelry and cash. The cops thought whoever was doing it was young—teenagers, or maybe early twenties. Maybe addicts looking for easy money for a quick fix. And that type of perpetrator would definitely panic and react ... well, badly, if they were surprised in the act."

"What about David? Did Detective Arnold have an opinion of him?" I asked.

"He did," Wyle acknowledged with a slight nod. "It wasn't entirely ... charitable. Although he, of course, didn't think David deserved to die, he wasn't completely surprised it happened."

"What do you mean?" I asked.

Wyle ate another bite of muffin. "Apparently, David was known for being a pain in the rear. Once he got an idea in his head, he was like a dog with a bone. He would charge ahead, determined to prove his theory, never mind who was hurt in the process."

"Sounds like he was a hit at parties," Pat said.

Wyle gave her a sideways smile. "Yeah, he wasn't terribly liked. Ike wasn't the first person David was convinced of being guilty of something, but David did seem to be more fixated on Ike than normal. Arnold thought David may have had a crush on Kat."

I thought about David and the way his voice had softened when he spoke about her. "Yeah, I can see that."

Wyle glanced at me. "Did he say anything to you about having feelings for her?"

"Not in so many words, but his demeanor definitely changed when he spoke about her."

"Did Kat return his feelings?" Pat asked.

I frowned. "I doubt it. Kat seemed pretty taken with Ike."

"Maybe that's the real reason behind David's single-minded focus on Ike," Pat said. "If he wanted Kat for himself, then getting Ike sent to jail would be a great way to remove him from the picture."

"That's exactly what Arnold thought," Wyle said.

"I don't know," I said. "That doesn't feel right to me."

"But you just said you thought David might have had a thing for Kat," Pat said.

"I don't know if I would go that far," I said. "It's true I wouldn't be surprised to find out if he did. But I don't think that was the only thing driving David. What about that aunt ... the one Ike supposedly killed?"

"Ah, yes, Arnold mentioned that," Wyle said. "David apparently filed a report about his aunt's death, claiming it was suspicious."

"And was it?"

"Arnold didn't think so. David's aunt wasn't healthy. She had multiple issues, including dementia. While it does seem to be true that she lost her money, it's not clear that Ike had anything to do with it."

"Had Ike met her?"

"It seems so. His aunt contacted Ike because she thought she was being haunted by her husband's ghost, so he did investigate. But there's no record of him getting any more than his normal fee."

"Hmm," I said. "You know, this would all make more sense if Ike was the one who had been murdered rather than David."

"Why? Ike could have killed David because he was sick of being persecuted by him," Wyle said.

"Maybe," I said. "But something doesn't seem right. Did Arnold have an opinion of Ike?"

Wyle raised his eyebrows. "Well, it's funny you should ask. Arnold did have some interesting things to say about him."

"Like?"

"Like how nervous Ike was when they questioned him about Abe's death."

"So, Ike WAS a suspect?" I asked.

"Not officially," Wyle said. "But after David put up such a stink, they decided to ask Ike a few questions. Ike and Kat did work together, so his being involved wasn't out of the realm of possibility."

"What did Ike say?"

"Not much, other than he and Kat were friends. But he had never met Abe. When they asked him where he was the night of Abe's murder, he said he was home alone."

"Home alone?" I asked. "Not with Kat?"

Wyle eyed me. "Was he supposed to be with Kat?"

"Well, Kat says he was," I said. "That they were ... together the night Abe was killed."

"Maybe that's why he was nervous," Wyle said. "He was with Kat but didn't want to admit it."

"Possible," I said. "Where did Kat say she was that night?"

"Working late. She had a couple of meetings after school and stayed late to grade papers and set up her classroom for the next day. According to Kat, she wasn't in any rush to get home, as she thought Abe would be working late, as well. So, she was shocked when she walked in and found him."

"Do you think she was lying? And she was really with Ike?" Pat asked.

"It's possible. According to Kat, Ike didn't want the cops to know they were involved. He thought that would make them more suspicious of him," I said. "So, maybe they were both lying about where they were that night."

"I don't know if lying about it worked either," Wyle said. "Arnold definitely had his radar up around Ike—and not just because of how he reacted to being questioned, but in general. This idea of taking money to investigate so-called hauntings didn't sit well with Arnold. I guess despite living in Sleepy Hollow, he isn't much of a believer in ghosts.

"Still, there was no proof Ike was anywhere near the house. Nor could they find any motive for why Ike would kill Abe, as they didn't seem to know that Kat and Ike were more than friends. Other than thinking Ike was a bit of a con man and how he acted a little too nervous when he was questioned, there was really no reason to investigate him."

"Did David give the detectives any reason to suspect Ike? Other than what happened to his aunt?" I asked.

"That was strange, too," Wyle said. "David did say he had proof that tied Ike to the scene of the crime that night, but he wouldn't tell the detectives what it was. He just kept saying if they dug into the case enough, they would find it themselves, and that he wasn't paid to do their work for them. You can imagine that didn't sit well with anyone, but Arnold did say he went over his files and notes again just to humor the guy and found nothing."

"He's probably talking about the so-called witness who saw Ike that night," I said. "Although at this point, I'm thinking David was the witness, but he didn't want to admit that he was, in essence, stalking Ike."

"I'm inclined to agree with you," Wyle said.

"Why wouldn't David want to tell them what he found?" Pat asked. "I mean, if he was the witness and didn't live in the neighborhood, I get why he didn't tell the cops. But what reason did he give the cops for not telling them?"

Wyle tossed the last of his muffin into his mouth and wiped his fingers on a napkin. "David made a few comments about corruption and not knowing who to trust. Again, that didn't sit particularly well with anyone, especially since the department had always taken David's accusations seriously in the past and done what they could to investigate them."

"Boy, Detective Arnold wasn't kidding," Pat said. "At this point, I'm surprised David wasn't murdered sooner."

"What about Ike disappearing?" I asked. "Did you mention that to Detective Arnold? Did he have any thoughts about it?"

"That bothered him, too," Wyle said. "He found it odd that Ike just up and left Sleepy Hollow the way he did. There's no law against an adult going wherever he wants, of course, but he found the timing interesting. The moment the case was closed, Ike gave notice and left."

"How did Detective Arnold even know?" I asked. "Was he keeping tabs on Ike?"

"David told him," Wyle said grimly. "David made a point of telling the Sleepy Hollow Police Department how they had made a huge mistake in not charging Ike and letting him get away."

"I guess that means Detective Arnold doesn't think anything happened to Ike, then," I said.

Wyle picked up his mug. "Anything is possible, but the circumstances are pretty coincidental. And Arnold doesn't seem to be a man who believes in coincidences."

"Does he think Ike is guilty?" Pat asked.

"Not in so many words. But, yeah, it sure seems like Ike is guilty of something."

I reached for a muffin, my mind whirling as all the different pieces tried to fit into place. But no matter how I put them together, nothing was making sense.

"How about the Headless Horseman?" Pat asked. "Did you ask Detective Arnold about that?"

"I asked him about the pranks, yes," Wyle said. "He isn't aware of any of that happening in Sleepy Hollow."

"That sort of blows up the theory that the Headless Horseman is haunting Ike," Pat mused. "You'd think it would have started in Sleepy Hollow, if it were true. Unless ..." Pat's eyes brightened. "Maybe the Headless Horseman was so unhappy Ike left, he decided to follow him."

Wyle shot Pat a look. "Yes, I'm sure that's what happened."

"All that aside," I said, shooting them both a look, "what about me? As of right now, *The Redemption Times* has outed me as a suspect in this murder investigation. What should I do?"

"Nothing," Wyle said immediately as he got to his feet. "You stay out of sight for the moment. I'm going to pay a visit to Tad to find out who his source is."

"He probably won't tell you," Pat said. "He'll claim confidentiality or some such nonsense."

"He can claim that, but that won't protect him from being sued for libel," Wyle said. "If the police department isn't backing up his claim that you're about to be arrested, he's going to have to answer for this."

"The problem is, he doesn't actually say I'm about to be arrested," I said, picking up the paper. "He just says I was questioned by the police, which I was. I know it feels like that's the point of the story, but he never actually says it directly."

"Well, you're a private citizen, so he does have to be careful," Wyle said. "And he knows it. So, I think I can rattle his cage a bit. But ..." He glared meaningfully at me. "You need to stay out of sight. Let me handle it."

"But ..." I started to protest, but Wyle was shaking his head.

"No 'buts,'" he said. "I'll see what I can get out of Tad, but the last thing you need is any other legal issues, so it's best if you just stay out of it. You don't say anything to Tad that can be used against you. Got it?"

What Wyle said made sense, logically. But the idea of me being trapped in my home unable to defend myself from false accusations set my teeth on edge. However, one look at the set expression on Wyle's face made me realize that arguing with him would get me nowhere. "Fine," I sighed.

He flashed me a crooked smile. "Don't look so defeated. Trust me … it's better this way."

"Yeah. I'm sure you're right," I said as Wyle headed out the door.

Neither Pat nor I said anything until we heard the click of the door closing. "I don't know why he's bothering with Tad," Pat said. "I'm sure this is all Louise."

I cupped my hands around my coffee mug. The more I thought about sitting inside my house stewing while people perpetuated the rumor about me killing someone, the less I liked it. While there was no question I trusted Wyle—I was sure he would do everything he could to keep me out of jail—it wasn't like I was his only case. It was quite possible his boss might decide to rearrange his priorities, and who knew when he would be able to fit me in?

On top of that, the fact that there might be some officers who were also glad I was home twiddling my thumbs made me wonder how motivated the department was to have Wyle sort it out. Worse, maybe it would never be sorted out. Not that I thought it would go so far as to land me in jail, but if my name was never cleared, then perhaps I would be less likely to meddle in future investigations.

It was a dark thought—that some people might be happy if my reputation was ruined just to keep themselves from being embarrassed. But now that it had occurred to me, I couldn't stop thinking about it.

And the more I thought about it, the more I realized I needed to do something about it.

"Maybe we need to go find out if that's true," I said.

Pat looked at me in surprise. "But didn't Wyle just tell you to stay put?"

"He told me not to call Tad," I said, standing up. "And I'm not. I'm talking to another private citizen. Want to come?"

A slow smile spread across Pat's face as she got to her feet. "Are you kidding? I wouldn't miss this for the world."

Chapter 19

Pat looked over at me. "Ready?" Tiki's head popped out of Pat's purse, an inquiring expression on her face, as well.

We were standing on Louise's front porch. I hadn't been there in years, since I had first moved to town, but nothing had changed. The same cheery welcome mat sat in front of the door, the same hanging pots, now filled with dead flowers, hung from the rafters, and the same white wicker chair was in the corner. My heart ached as I remembered a happier time when Louise would be excited to see me on her front porch instead of the negative reaction I would likely be greeted with now.

I took a deep breath and steeled myself. It had to be done.

"Ready," I said.

I stepped to the side, leaving Pat in front of the peephole. I wasn't trying to necessarily hide from Louise, but I thought she might be more inclined to open the door for Pat than she would for me.

Pat rang the doorbell. I heard the sound of light, excited footsteps running toward the door, followed by slower, heavier ones.

There were sounds of a bit of a scuffle along with the protesting voice of a child before the door swung open. Louise stood there, holding her daughter Jessica on one hip. Louise's blonde hair was greasy and falling out of its rough ponytail. Her oversized sweatshirt was stained, and she had no makeup covering the dark circles under her eyes. In contrast, Jessica, her two-year-old toddler, was bright and happy-looking with her shiny blonde curls, big blue eyes, and red dress sporting a smiling elephant.

Louise's face instantly soured when she recognized us. "Oh, I should have known this day could get worse," she snapped as Jessica's entire face lit up.

"Doggy," she cried, reaching her little hands toward Tiki.

"No doggy," Louise said, slapping down the little girl's hands. "I don't have time for this," she said to us. "As you can see, I'm busy."

"It will only take a moment," I said.

"I don't have a moment," Louise said.

"Doggy!" Jessica squealed again.

"No doggy," Louise repeated.

"Her name is Tiki," Pat said to Jessica. "If you're very gentle, you can pet her. If your mother will let you, that is."

A wide smile split Jessica's face, and she jumped up and down in Louise's arms. Louise shot Pat a murderous look. Pat smiled at her sweetly. "It's only a couple of questions," Pat said. "It won't take long, and Jessica can pet Tiki."

"Fine," Louise said, her voice irritated as she deposited the child on the ground. Pat knelt down, and Tiki immediately started licking Jessica's hands. She giggled.

Louise looked down at her daughter, an unreadable expression on her face, before turning to me. "What do you want?" she asked, folding her arms across her chest.

"Why did you warn me about staying away from David?"

Louise rolled her eyes. "Oh, you're back on that again?"

"Yes, I am. Because to me, it looks like you knew that David was going to be murdered."

"How on Earth would I know that?"

"That's an excellent question. How WOULD you know that?"

Louise put a hand on her hip. "I don't know what you're talking about. I had no idea David would be murdered."

"Then why did you warn me to stay away from him?"

Her eyes narrowed as she glared at me. "I don't have to answer to you."

"That's true, you don't," I said. "But the cops are a different story."

She didn't immediately respond, instead twisting her mouth like she was trying to sort out how best to answer. I had no doubt that she really wanted to tell me to get lost, but in the back of her head, she was also probably wondering just how much trouble she was about to find herself in with the cops.

"Fine," she said at last. "If you must know, it was Kat."

"Kat? She told you David would be murdered?"

Louise looked at me in disgust. "No! Of course not. She was the one who told me David was bad news, and I should stay away."

"And you, out of the goodness of your heart, decided to share that with me." My voice was heavy with sarcasm.

But Louise surprised me. "It wasn't actually my idea," she said. "It was Kat's."

"Kat told you to warn me to stay away?" I couldn't hide the surprise in my voice.

"Not in so many words. She said David was bad news and someone really ought to warn you about him. As a good neighbor, I took it upon myself to be the one to do it."

I didn't believe the good neighbor stuff for a moment. I figured the only reason she said something was to try and get under my skin, and then the whole situation blew up in a way even she couldn't have predicted. "How did you meet Kat, anyway?"

"She was lost and asked me for directions. I told her I'd walk her, and we struck up a conversation and ended up hanging out a few times." Louise's expression was faintly defensive. "She was lonely. What she was doing was tough, trying to track down her love. Especially when her family all thought she was crazy to be chasing after him the way she was."

"Why would her family think that?"

"Because they didn't approve. They thought it unseemly." Louise shook her head. "It was too soon after Abe's death. They thought she should properly mourn him before running off after another guy. They didn't understand the relationship with Abe was over even if he hadn't been killed."

I opened my mouth, about to say something about Abe being an abuser, then closed it again. It suddenly occurred to me that Wyle hadn't said anything about Abe being an abuser, either. Maybe Kat never filed a report with the Sleepy Hollow

Police Department. A lot of abused wives never tell anyone, but still. I found it odd that Kat told me but not Louise.

"Are we done?" Louise asked. "Have I sufficiently answered your questions?"

"Yes, and I appreciate it," I said as Pat gently extracted Tiki from Jessica's hands, much to the little girl's chagrin. Jessica opened her mouth to protest.

"That's enough doggy," Louise said before glaring at Pat. "Thanks for nothing."

"Nice seeing you, too," Pat said cheerily as we walked away. I heard Jessica wail before Louise slammed the door shut.

"What do you think?" I asked Pat.

Pat glanced behind her. "I think I feel sorry for Jessica." She shook her head sadly. "Louise was never keen on being a mother. Bill was the one who pushed her. I think if she had just stuck with the one, it would have been fine, but having Jessica … and right after her brother disappearing? I just don't see this having a good end."

"I don't disagree, but I was thinking more about what Louise said about Kat and David," I said.

Pat flashed me a sideways smile. "Oh, that. On the surface, it makes sense. Does it jive with what you've heard from Kat? I've never met her, so I don't know."

"Yes and no," I said slowly, the wheels turning in my head. "I am starting to realize no one has talked to Kat yet. Nor does it seem like she's on anyone's radar."

"Yes, that is a bit surprising," Pat agreed.

Chapter 20

"Charlie! It's so great to see you." Kat smiled as she approached me in the lobby of the Redemption Inn.

After some discussion with Pat, I had dropped her off. She wasn't terribly happy about it, as she would have preferred to come with me, but as I explained, Kat didn't know her at all and would likely not open up if Pat was with me.

Pat reluctantly agreed, but only after I promised to call her the moment I was done.

I went to the Redemption Inn hoping against hope that Kat would be in her room, or if she wasn't, that maybe Nancy would know where she was. Instead, I found her in the lobby.

"I was hoping to run into you," I said. "Are you going somewhere?"

"I was just going to take a walk. I need to … get some air."

"Of course," I said. "Would you like some company?"

Her eyes widened in surprise. "Ah, sure."

I cocked my head. "You don't have to say yes if you don't want to."

"No, no." She seemed flustered again. "It's not that. Sure. I'd love the company."

"Great." We started walking toward the front door. Inside, I mentally crossed my fingers, hoping I wouldn't run into anyone I knew. Especially Wyle, after I told him I wouldn't do anything more to involve myself.

We stepped out and started walking up the street. The air was crisp, and the sun was beginning to set.

"How are you doing?" I asked.

She glanced at me in surprise. "I feel like I should be asking you that."

"Why?"

"Because I think I owe you an apology."

Now it was my turn to look at her in surprise. "Why?" The folded note on my porch popped into my brain. *I'm sorry.* Was Kat the one who sent it?

She waved her hands. "I sort of feel like this is all my fault."

"What's your fault?"

"You getting in trouble with the cops." She gave me a sheepish grin. "I feel like I should have warned you about David, and then maybe you could have, I don't know, stayed away from him."

"Well, I don't think there's anything you have to be sorry about," I said.

She glanced up at me sideways. "I appreciate that."

We walked a few more steps as I watched her out of the corner of my eye. She seemed to relax the longer we walked. "But back to you … is everything okay?"

She shot me a quick glance. "Why wouldn't it be?"

"You're just acting a little … strange. And I wasn't sure if there was a reason why you wanted a walk. Like you're having a bad day or something."

She went back to staring at the ground. "Oh, well, I'm worried about Ike."

"You haven't seen him at all?"

She shook her head. "And it's just so unlike him. Something must have happened to him. I've called all the hospitals around here again today, asking if anyone who matches his description has been admitted, but I keep getting the runaround. It's so frustrating."

"Have you talked to the cops?"

She snorted in disgust. "Every day. It doesn't matter. No one has any information at all. I even started …" She took a deep breath and seemed close to tears. "I even started calling the local morgues."

I shot her a quick look. "I take it there has been no sign of him there, either?"

"No. Which is good, of course. I mean, I of course don't want him to be dead. It's just so frustrating. Where is he? None of this makes sense." She ground her teeth together.

We passed a local boutique that had set out a couple of gaily carved jack-o'-lanterns next to the front door. They gave me the creeps, and I immediately turned my head away while simultaneously feeling a jolt of anger that a couple of pranks had ruined jack-o'-lanterns for me. "How does Ike get from city to city?" I asked, even though I knew the answer.

She glanced at me. "He drives. That's easiest for him. Then he doesn't have to worry about planes and renting cars."

"And his car is still here?"

"Of course."

"How about you?"

"What do you mean?"

"How have you been following him?"

"I've been driving, too," she said. "It's even more difficult for me, as I have no idea when he's going to leave or where he's going, so I have to be even more flexible."

"And how are you keeping track of where he's going?" I asked. "I assume with your private detective's help?"

"Yes. I couldn't do it without him."

"And how does your private detective track Ike down?" I asked.

Kat glanced at me, a crease between her eyes. "I have no idea. If I knew how he was doing it, I wouldn't need him."

"What about David?"

Kat's steps started to slow down. "What about David?"

"How was David tracking Ike?"

"I don't know. Why are you asking me all these questions?" Her voice was edging on hysteria.

I paused in the street and stared at her, the pieces finally falling into place. "David was your private detective, wasn't he?"

She had taken a few steps forward before pausing and turning to face me, as well. "David was an investigative reporter."

"An investigative reporter could easily moonlight as a private detective," I said. "Even if he was doing it unofficially."

"But David was trying to persecute the man I love. Why would I work with him?"

"Because you needed someone to help you find Ike," I said. "You couldn't do it alone. And David WAS finding him, wasn't he? He was behind the jack- o'-lanterns and horse galloping, after all. He was trying to drive Ike mad, so he would confess."

"I don't know what you're talking about," she said, but the color had drained from her face. "David was the one who was mad, not Ike. I already told you how David was completely irrational when it came to Ike."

"Which is why he was also easy to manipulate, wasn't he? You gave him some sob story about being another one of Ike's victims and needing to find him for some reason, and David was only too happy to oblige." My mind was shuffling back through all my encounters with Kat, David, and Ike, and it was all becoming clear.

"That first time we were sitting in the lobby ... that was David you saw, wasn't it?" The brief glimpse of the stooped-shouldered man with the graying hair disappearing up the stairs. The only reason why I had turned to see him was because Kat was leaving in a huff. "Although ..." I cocked my head, remembering the anger on Kat's face before she ran off. "I don't understand why you were so upset with him. Was he not supposed to be staying at the same hotel as you, or something?"

"This is absurd," she said through gritted teeth. "I don't have to listen to this."

I snapped my fingers. "No, the problem was, it was the same hotel *Ike* was staying at, wasn't it? If David was there as well, that would complicate things. If David found you with Ike, or vice versa, you'd have a lot of explaining to do, playing both sides like that."

"I wasn't trying to play both sides. David shouldn't have been there at all. None of this is my fault."

"Your fault?" I stared at her in disbelief. "Who said any of this was your fault?"

"I said it's NOT my fault."

"What's not your fault?"

Her hands fluttered around her head. "Any of it. What happened to David."

I could feel my jaw drop open even as I tried to control my expression. It all made sense now. "You killed David, didn't you?"

Her eyes widened as her face went from red to white again, except for two bright-red spots on her cheeks. "I did no such thing," she gasped.

"Why did you do it, Kat? Was it because Ike disappeared, and you blamed David?"

"Ike *loves* me," she said. "We're soulmates. He would *never* disappear if he knew I was here. David messed things up somehow. Of course Ike didn't want to have anything to do with David, and I don't blame him. David wanted to ruin his life!"

For a moment, I was speechless. Kat had transformed before my eyes. She was like a crazy woman, her fists clenched and eyes wild.

How could I have missed the instability in her? It was so clear. This was no love triangle ... it was an obsession—*her* obsession.

"Are you sure Ike loves you?" I asked, my voice careful as I took a step back from her. We were outside in the middle of the sidewalk, surrounded by businesses and storefronts, although some were already closed. And while there weren't a lot of people walking around, cars continued passing by. It was getting darker as the sun began to set, but there was still plenty of light. Not to mention she was a lot smaller than me. I figured if she rushed me, I could easily hold her off.

Unless she had a weapon.

I put that thought aside. I would deal with it if it happened.

Kat seemed to get even crazier. "Of course he loved me!" she shrieked. "Haven't you been listening to me?"

I took another step back. "I have. Maybe we need a break. Should we go back to the Redemption Inn? We could get some coffee or tea. Nancy probably has some of her famous cookies out, as well ..."

"I don't want cookies," she snarled, her eyes narrowing. Her expression changed, turned more cunning. "You're trying to trick me, aren't you? You killed David, and you're trying to pin it all on me."

"No, no, no. I wouldn't dream of doing that."

"But you just said you thought I was the one who killed David."

"I was mistaken," I said, trying to will her to calm down. I couldn't believe how suddenly empty the streets were. How could there be no one walking by? "I just figured the most important thing we can do right now is focus on finding Ike."

"Yes, *I* need to focus on finding Ike," she said. "There's no 'we' here. I know you were trying to steal him away from me, but ..."

"Whoa," I interrupted, putting both hands up, palms out, as I took another step backward. My eyes darted around, hoping I could catch a glimpse of someone—anyone—nearby. "I wasn't trying to steal anyone away from anything."

"Yes, you were," she said. "I saw the look in your eyes when his name came up."

"That's not true," I said. "There was no look in my eyes. None."

"You were trying to date him," she said, her eyes glittering with anger. "You showed up at the hotel looking for him."

"I did, but not to date him."

"I don't believe you," she said. "You wanted him. But he's *mine*."

"Let's go back to the hotel, and we can talk about it."

She stared at me, and I could almost see the wheels turning in her head. "Did YOU do something to Ike? Were you so jealous you couldn't have him that you killed him?"

"*What?*"

"That's it, isn't it? You wanted him, but he didn't want you, so you killed him. And David found out about it, and you killed him, too."

"Kat, none of that is true."

She paused then and smiled at me. A cold, cruel smile. "Oh, it will be true. By the time I'm done."

I felt a chill run down my spine. I opened my mouth to respond, but at that moment, I heard a voice. "That's enough," Wyle said, emerging from the side alley. "Kat, I think you need to come with me."

My knees went weak with relief. I was never so glad to see anyone in my life. Kat, on the other hand, looked panicked. Her jaw dropped, and her eyes jerked from me to him. "But officer, it's all her," she pointed at me. "She confessed to killing David. You have to arrest her."

"Uh huh," Wyle said. "Let's talk about it at the station." Turning to me, he muttered, "We'll talk later."

Even though I was so relieved to see him, I also felt a tiny jolt of "oh crap." I was probably in for one heck of a lecture.

But in this case, he might have a point.

Chapter 21

"I still can't believe it was all Kat," Pat said. We were sitting in my kitchen with cups of tea and a plate of frosted brownies in front of us. After the week I had, I figured I was entitled.

"Well, it wasn't just Kat," I said. "She was definitely the mastermind behind the pranks, even though David was the one doing them."

"But she killed David," Pat said, reaching for a brownie. Tiki's nose followed Pat's hand. Today, Tiki was dressed in a black sweater with a smiling white ghost saying "boo" on it. I didn't even want to think about all the Christmas sweaters that dog was going to own before all was said and done.

"That seems to be what the evidence is pointing to," I said. Kat, for her part, had not confessed yet and was still insisting I was the one who had killed David. Unfortunately for her, there was no evidence I had been in David's hotel room, but there *was* evidence that Kat had been, which was why Wyle had showed up when he did. He had been looking for Kat to bring her in for questioning. The cops had found her fingerprints scattered throughout David's hotel room, which she insisted proved nothing other than that she had a conversation with him at one point in his room. The cops then found one of her shirts and a pair of jeans stuffed in the trash bin at the back of Redemption Inn. They were both covered with blood.

Kat had lawyered up at that point.

Pat shook her head. "It makes you wonder who else she's killed."

"You mean like Abe?"

Pat widened her eyes. "The fiancé? Oh man, I had forgotten about him. I was thinking Ike."

"You think she killed Ike?"

"Well, he is still missing."

Pat wasn't the only one who thought that. Wyle told me the police had doubled their search efforts for Ike, focusing now on the woods and the lake. Not that anyone held much hope of finding Ike if Kat had dumped him in the lake, as Angel's Lake rarely gave up its dead.

I wasn't as convinced. There were too many things that didn't add up. It had also come out that Kat had been the one calling me and hanging up. It seemed like she had been trying to frame me for David's death even before her confession in the street. All the little things she had been doing—befriending Louise to learn more about me, calling both Tad and the cops to provide anonymous tips about my being involved. She was convinced I was trying to steal Ike from her and was determined to prevent that.

Would she have done all of that if Ike was dead?

Not to mention how frantic she had become when she talk-ed about looking for Ike. Unless she was a superb actress, which was possible, or she was suffering from sort of mental disorder where she truly didn't remember killing Ike, I didn't think she had anything to do with his disappearance.

"I think it's more likely she was somehow involved with Abe's death than whatever happened to Ike," I said.

"What, you think there's a quota?" Pat asked. "The most likely scenario is that she was involved in all three deaths."

As much as I agreed with this theory making the most sense on the surface, there was something about it that didn't sit right with me. I just wasn't sure what it was.

* * *

I was cleaning up the kitchen after Pat left when the door-bell rang.

I froze, washcloth poised above the counter, a jolt of fear flooding my body. Almost immediately, I put the washcloth down and forced myself to take a deep breath, feeling both silly and uneasy.

Get it together, Charlie. You're being foolish. Despite knowing without a shadow of a doubt that the jack-o'-lanterns and horse galloping were pranks, and that the two people responsible were either dead or in jail, the sound of an unexpected doorbell still made me flinch.

Hopefully, that reaction wouldn't last long. Although I guessed I shouldn't find it surprising that it was taking some time to get over, as there were still a lot of unanswered questions floating around.

I went to the door and peeked through the peephole. A man wearing a baseball cap that shielded his face stood on my porch. With his head bowed, I couldn't get a good look at him. Although I didn't think I knew him, something tugged at me that he was familiar.

I opened the door. "Can I help you?"

The man slowly raised his head to meet my eyes. His hair was jet-black, and he had a matching thick mustache, so it took me a moment to recognize him. Still, I would have recognized the eyes behind the glasses anywhere.

My mouth dropped open. "*Ike?*"

He gave me a slight bow. "In the flesh."

"You're not ... what happened to you?"

He grimaced. "It's a long story. Do you have some time?"

"Of course." I held open the door wider so he could come in before leading him to the kitchen. "Tea?"

"Absolutely. I'm not about to turn down Charlie's famous tea."

"Ha," I said, as I headed into the kitchen.

He paused behind me. "Actually, do you mind if I use your bathroom first?"

"Of course. Just head back through to the living room and to your left."

He nodded slightly and turned away while I focused on making the tea.

I had it on the table, along with more brownies, when Ike reappeared looking like his old self. The mustache was gone, along with the black hair and baseball cap. He smiled self-consciously when he saw me and ran his hand through his sandy-brown hair, which was a much better match to his skin color.

"Much better," I said. "That color was dreadful on you."

His grin widened. "Trust me, it's a relief to get rid of that disguise. The mustache itched."

"I'll bet."

He moved to take a seat, deliberately not choosing the one with a book in front of it. While he was in the bathroom, I had dug it up and left it on the table for him.

"That's yours," I said, gesturing with my head as I brought the tea over.

He shot me a confused look before focusing on the cover. His eyes widened. "You bought it for me?"

"I did," I said, sitting across from him.

He looked into my eyes. "Thank you. This means a lot."

I waved him off, a little disconcerted by what I saw in his eyes. "Really not a big deal. Consider it my contribution to your Redemption research."

"I hope that won't be your only contribution," he said.

I gave him a slight shrug and picked up my tea. "We'll see." I kept my tone deliberately evasive, as the last thing I wanted to do was discourage him from answering my many questions.

He didn't push it. I watched him carefully place the book down next to him, keeping it away from his mug of tea.

The kitchen was warm and cozy, filled with the afternoon sun. Midnight was curled up in his normal chair by the window. He lazily lifted his head and blinked his emerald eyes at us before drifting back to sleep.

Ike picked up his mug but didn't drink. "Before I explain everything that's been happening, I owe you an apology."

I looked at him in surprise. "For what?"

He met my eyes then, his gaze intense. "For dragging you into this whole mess. I should have done something to stop it."

I stared at him for a moment as another piece fell into place. "The note," I said. "That was you apologizing?"

He nodded. "It was lame. I know it. But I felt like I had to do something. You were being railroaded, and there was nothing I could do to stop it."

I tilted my head. "Nothing you could do? If you knew something, you could have come out of hiding and told the police."

He made a face. "It wasn't quite that simple."

"Maybe you better explain."

He frowned at his tea. "I'm not even sure where to start."

"How about at the beginning?"

To my surprise, he laughed softly. "The beginning. Oh man." He covered his eyes with his hands. I stayed silent, giving him time to figure out how to begin.

Finally, he dropped his hands and straightened. "I guess the most obvious place to start is when Kat arrived, although I'm not sure if that's the actual beginning or not."

"What do you mean?"

He sighed. "I guess I just need to start talking, and hopefully, it will eventually make more sense. I met Kat after she moved to Sleepy Hollow with her fiancé, Abe. She and I were both teachers in the same school district."

He paused and began twisting his mug on the table. "Looking back, I feel like such an idiot. From the moment I met her, something felt ... wrong. The way she looked at me ... there was something predatory about it. Like she was a hungry tiger, and I was a gazelle. But I told myself I was being ridiculous. She was engaged, after all. I was letting my imagination run away from me. She just wanted to make some friends. She was lonely. Her fiancé worked long hours so, of course, she was looking for someone to talk to. And I became that someone.

"But the more I got to know her, the more uncomfortable I became. Her true intentions were becoming more and more clear—she wanted something more than a friend. But the thing is, even if she hadn't been involved with Abe, I wouldn't have been interested. The fact that she had a fiancé just made it a hard pass for me."

"What did you do?"

He shrugged. "What could I do? I let her down as gently as possible, telling her I couldn't even think of dating someone who was already involved with someone else. In retrospect, I think this was a mistake. I should have probably told her it wouldn't have mattered if she was with Abe or not, because I just wasn't interested. That would have been harsher, but maybe it would have prevented all this tragedy."

He was silent, turning his head to stare out the window, a pensive look on his face. I stayed quiet as well, sipping my tea and reaching for another brownie. What the heck … one more couldn't hurt.

"It was a Friday when I told her we could never be together. I didn't hear from her all weekend, and then she called in sick on Monday. I was a little concerned, wondering if maybe she was too embarrassed to face me, but mostly, I was just relieved to not have to deal with her.

"She was back on Tuesday, but she didn't look right. Her one eye was swollen, and she had on more makeup than normal. She told everyone she had tripped and ran into a doorway. Her fault. She was always so clumsy, she said. I thought that sounded strange, as I hadn't seen any signs of her being clumsy. It was later she confessed to me that Abe had hit her.

"Of course, I was horrified and told her she needed to go to the cops, but she refused, saying if she did, he would kill her. I told her she needed to leave him, but again, she said she couldn't. Not only would he come after her, but he'd seek out her family as well, and she just couldn't chance it.

"As you can imagine, none of that sat right with me, and I took it upon myself to do whatever I could to talk her out of staying with him." He paused and shook his head in disgust. "I was such a fool."

"Why?" I asked, although I had a feeling I knew what he was going to say. I could taste the bile rising in my throat. Kat had played me, just as she played Ike.

"She had made the whole thing up. She wasn't being abused."

His words hit me like a sledgehammer, even though I knew they were coming. "Are you sure about that?"

His voice was grim. "Positive. She made the whole thing up in order to get close to me. She was just manipulating me." His mouth twisted. "And I was an idiot to fall for it."

"You couldn't have known," I said, but my words felt hollow. Why hadn't *I* known? I had been abused—how on Earth had I not realized she was lying?

"Maybe. Maybe not. I don't know if I'm ready to let myself off the hook that easily. Anyway, after months of going back and forth on this, one night, she called me. She was hysterical. She had just found Abe, you see.

"I told her to call the police, and she said she already had, but she needed me there. She begged me to come over … said she really needed a friend while the cops were there. Like a fool, I told her I'd be right over, even though I knew in my gut it was a bad idea. I told myself there was nothing between us; we were just coworkers and friends, and even if the cops did look into our relationship, they wouldn't find anything.

"I had assumed the cops would be there when I arrived, but she was alone. She told me she was too upset to call them. I tried to do it myself, but she just broke down sobbing, and I ended up comforting her. Eventually, I calmed her enough where she agreed to call the cops.

"But by that time, I was even more uneasy at the idea of the cops finding the two of us there, alone with her dead fiancé. So, after she called, I told her I needed to leave. She was upset, but I explained there was going to be a lot of questions if I was there, and it would be better to leave me out of the story. It wasn't like I could add anything. I hadn't seen anything or been a witness to anything, and Kat would tell the cops what she told me. No harm, no foul.

"So of course, you can imagine my chagrin when David arrived at my house a few days later accusing me of killing Abe. The whole idea was absurd, and I told him so. But he said he had a witness who saw me leave Kat's house after Abe had been killed, and he was going to tell the cops. And who knew what would happen then?

"Well, not surprisingly, I panicked. I immediately went to find Kat. We needed a plan to get ahead of the whole thing. Imagine my surprise when Kat told me she had it handled, and everything would be fine ... but only if I would start dating her."

"She actually said that?" I was shocked, even though I told myself I shouldn't be. Kat standing in the street, threatening to tell the cops that I had confessed to killing David. Would she really stoop to any level?

"Not exactly," Ike said. "She would never say anything that blatant. But the meaning was clear. If I wanted to stay out of jail, she and I would need to get together. Otherwise, who knew what the cops would find out. After all, I had been there that night, right?"

"What did you do?"

"The only thing I could think of. I got out of Sleepy Hollow as fast as I could. In that moment, it was clear to me that Kat was obsessed with me, and I needed to get as far away from her as I possibly could. Luckily, I had just signed a contract with my publisher for this new book documenting hauntings in the Midwest. I had already been playing with the idea of taking a sabbatical for a semester to do the research, but that settled it. Within a few days, I had quit my job, packed my things, sublet my apartment, and left."

"But that wasn't the end of it, was it?"

He gave me a wry smile. "In retrospect, I probably should have known better, but at the time, I figured once I was gone, she would eventually move on. She had no ties to Sleepy Hollow, so why would she stay? Oh, sure, she would be initially upset, but once it was clear I wasn't coming back, she would go on with her life. I never dreamed she would come after me the way she did."

"When did you realize she was behind all the pranks?"

Ike ran a hand through hair as a faint flush stained his cheeks. "I started putting it all together a few days ago."

"So you really didn't know?"

He shook his head, the flush deepening. "I know. I know. I pride myself on being a skeptical ghost hunter, and I allowed myself to be taken in by such a silly prank. It truly never occurred to me that Kat and David would be behind such a thing. It wasn't until I saw her that day we were in the bookstore that it began to dawn on me what was really going on."

"That's why you ran off the way you did?" I saw him again in my mind, all the color blanched from his face, his eyes not on me, but looking off in the distance.

He ducked his head, apparently too embarrassed to meet my eyes. "I just panicked when I saw her. I didn't know what to do. All I could think was that I had to get out of there before she saw me. So, I ducked out of the back of the bookstore and ran to the hotel. But by the time I arrived, I started to realize that if she knew I was in Redemption—and why would she be in Redemption if she wasn't looking for me?—she probably knew where I was staying, as well. I was going to have to disappear. Again.

"So, I ran up to my room, threw a few things into a backpack ... nothing much, mind you. I wanted people to think I disappeared, not just checked out and left."

"Where did you go?"

His look was sheepish. "To Lee's."

"Lee knew about this?"

His eyes widened, and he shook his head firmly. "No! She didn't know anything about it."

"I don't understand. You were staying with her?"

He rubbed his jaw, avoiding my eyes again. "You know how she has that apartment above the garage? It's empty. Well, not completely. She was using it for storage. She gave me a key, so I could go in and out while doing my research. It was too hard for her to climb the steps, you see. So, she told me to just keep the key until I was done. No one was using it anyway."

"So, you just ... moved in?"

"Basically. I couldn't think of anywhere else to go. It was only going to be for a day or so, until I could figure out what to do." He gestured to the wig and mustache that was sitting on the table next to him. "I found these in one of the boxes and borrowed them."

"Wow." I couldn't think of what to say. "Lee didn't notice?"

He shook his head. "I was careful when I came and left, so no."

"But what have you been doing all this time?"

His mouth flattened. "Investigating. Initially, my thought was to leave again. Just ditch my things and take off. But then I realized how futile that would be. She had already found me once; did I really think she was going to give up now? And how exactly was I going to leave if most of my things and my car were still at the Redemption Inn? No, I was going to have to figure out a way to clear my name if I wanted to get out of this mess.

"So, I did some digging. I thought maybe it was time I discovered who exactly Kat is. But what I discovered ..." His jaw tightened. "Basically, everything she ever told me about her history was a lie."

"Like how Abe abused her."

He nodded. "That and everything else. I talked to multiple people about Abe, including his former girlfriends. Everyone agrees he was a sweetheart and would never strike a woman."

"That doesn't mean he wasn't an abuser, though," I said, remembering how my former fiancé had fooled a lot of people, too.

"No. It doesn't. But after I heard the whole story, and considering my own dealings with Kat, I was more inclined to believe them. Abe had money. His family owns a very successful business, and Abe co-managed it with his brother. It wasn't easy for Abe to move to Sleepy Hollow and still work in the business, but Kat insisted, and according to everyone, whatever Kat wanted, Kat got. So, they moved, and Abe did what he could remotely along with some commuting."

"I don't get it," I said. "Why did Kat want to move to Sleepy Hollow?"

Ike stared at me, his eyes bitter. "Don't you see? Because of me."

My mouth fell open. "You? How did that happen? I thought you said you first met her in Sleepy Hollow?"

"Because that was the first time I remember meeting her, but apparently, that wasn't the first time we met," he said. "It was a couple of years ago when my first book was published, and my publishers booked me on a signing tour. I don't remember meeting her, but I guess she had showed up to one of my book signings. And ..." he held his hands up helplessly.

I stared at him, aghast. "That was it? This whole obsession started because of a book signing?"

"Apparently. According to one of her friends, she couldn't stop talking about me from then on."

"But ... why didn't she leave Abe?"

"I'm sure because of his money. She's the beneficiary of his will, you know."

My eyes widened as a few more pieces clicked into place. "You don't think she ..."

"Was responsible for Abe's death? I absolutely think she was. I think she planned it all. Whether or not she actually did the deed or not, I'm not sure, but yes, I think she planned everything. Including the robberies that took place before his murder, so the cops wouldn't think twice about their house being robbed."

"That's just ... shocking." That word didn't seem adequate for what Kat had done, the destruction she had caused, and the lives she had ruined, but it was the first to pop into my head.

Ike nodded again, his eyes now fixed on mine. "That's Kat."

Chapter 22

I finished parking the car in front of the small, neat house at the end of a street. My hands were sweaty, and I rubbed them on my jeans as I stared at Wyle's house. I had never been to it before.

The one part of Kat's story that still bothered me was why she killed David. Ike hadn't known for sure, but if he had to guess, he thought it was because Kat no longer needed his services, now that she had found Ike in Redemption, and David knew more than Kat was comfortable with. Or more likely, she was unable to control David anymore. David was becoming more and more unhinged when it came to Ike, and it was possible that he had no intention of stopping his quest to see Ike behind bars. Kat might have decided she had no choice but to kill him.

As Ike was leaving, he tried one more time to get me to agree to letting him feature my home in his book. "It won't be complete without Helen Blackstone's house," he had said again.

I smiled and shook my head. "Sorry. It's just not possible. For a lot of reasons."

"There's nothing I can say to convince you?"

"Alas, no."

He flashed his most charming smile then. "How about just dinner? My treat for everything I put you through? It's the least I could do."

There was no mistaking his message or the look in his eyes. I found myself thinking about Pat and what she had said about me using Ike to keep a wall between Wyle and me, and I shook my head. "I appreciate that, but it's not necessary."

His smile dimmed. "Ah, it's the cop then, after all."

It was on the tip of my tongue to tell him absolutely not—that my relationship with Wyle was strictly platonic—but I closed my mouth firmly. "Yes. It's complicated, but ... yes."

He reached out to put a gentle hand on my arm. "You don't have to explain. I get complicated. Wyle is a lucky guy."

"Actually, I don't know how lucky he is," I said.

Ike's smile was a bittersweet. "Trust me. He's lucky."

Now, standing in front of Wyle's house, I still didn't agree with Ike. I wasn't sure Wyle would agree either. But I definitely thought I owed him something.

I wiped my damp hands on my jeans one more time and slid out of the car. It was starting to get dark, as the sun was fading behind the trees. I wasn't even sure if he was home or not, but I thought I'd give it a shot.

I moved up the small walkway to the front porch, rang the doorbell, and waited. It took a few minutes—long enough for me to think maybe he wasn't home, after all. Even though it was starting to get cold, I was feeling feverish with nerves.

When he finally opened his door, he looked surprised to see me. "Charlie. Is something wrong? Do you want to come in?" He had on tight jeans and a faded blue sweatshirt, and he was holding a bottle of beer.

I shook my head. "I just ... I don't need to come in. I just had something I wanted to say."

"Okay," he said, his voice cautious, and he stepped out onto the porch with me, closing the door behind him. "What is it?"

I stared up at him, into those dark-brown eyes, and took a deep breath. "I'm not who you think I am," I said, my words coming out in a rush.

A hint of a smile crossed his lips. "How do you know who I think you are?"

"I just ... there's things about me you don't know."

He cocked his head as he studied me. "You don't think I know that? I'm a cop. It's what I do."

"Yes, but ... it's complicated."

"Again, you're not telling me anything I don't know. Where is this coming from?"

I took a deep breath. "Look. There are things about me ... I was in an abusive relationship. I just ... it's complicated."

I was still stuttering when Wyle reached out a hand and squeezed my arm. "Hey," he said, his voice gentle. I stopped talking and met his eyes. "It's okay. You can tell me when you're ready. And I hope one day, you will trust me enough with your secrets. But until then, it's okay. There are things ... well, it's complicated on my end, too. There's something going on at the station that I haven't figured out yet, and if we were to date, well that would make things even more awkward than they already are. Do you understand?"

I stared into his eyes, disappointment and relief jumbled together inside me. I knew it would never work out between us—it *couldn't* work out between us—and yet ... I wished things were different. Staring into his eyes, I could see he felt the same.

I nodded. "Yes. I completely understand."

A Word From Michele

Can't get enough of Charlie? I've got you covered. Keep going with book 6, *Red Hot Murder*.

One night, one of Charlie's customers passes out, only to wake up to her fiancé dead in her home and no memory of what happened the night before.

She swears the only thing she drank was a cup of Charlie's tea.

Charlie knows it wasn't the tea, but everyone else is suddenly blaming her, so she has no choice but to get to the bottom of this mysterious death.

Grab your copy right here:

amazon.com/dp/B0BFC7MN2G

* * *

You can also check out exclusive bonus content for The Murder of Sleepy Hollow including an epilogue between Kat and Charlie. Here's the link:

MPWNovels.com/r/q/sleepyhollow-bonus

The bonus content reveals hints, clues, and sneak peeks you won't get just by reading the books, so you'll definitely want to check it out. You're going to discover a side of Redemption that is only available here:

* * *

If you enjoyed The Murder of Sleepy Hollow, it would be wonderful if you would take a few minutes to leave a review and rating on Amazon: amazon.com/gp/product/B09YDQ2NF4/#customerReviews or Goodreads: goodreads.com/book/show/62564322-the-murder-of-sleepy-hollow or Bookbub: www.bookbub.com/books/the-murder-of-sleepy-hollow-charlie-kingsley-mysteries-book-5-by-michele-pw-pariza-wacek

(Feel free to follow me on any of those platforms as well.) I thank you and other readers will thank you (as your reviews will help other readers find my books.)

The *Charlie Kingsley Mysteries* series is a spin-off from my award-winning *Secrets of Redemption* series. *Secrets of Redemption* is a little different from the *Charlie Kingsley Mysteries,* as it's more psychological suspense, but it's still clean like a cozy.

You can learn more about both series, including how they fit together, at MPWNovels.com, along with lots of other fun things such as short stories, deleted scenes, giveaways, recipes, puzzles and more.

I've also included a sneak peek of, *Red Hot Murder*, if you'd like to check it out. Just turn the page to get started.

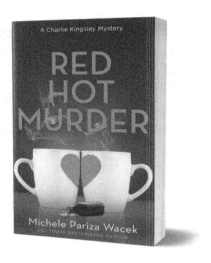

Red Hot Murder - Chapter 1

"Charlie, you are a lifesaver," Cherry gushed as I handed her a bag of tea. "I don't even want to think about what I would have done if I had run out."

"I'm glad I didn't let you down," I said, trying to keep my face composed. Cherry was a good customer and fun to talk to, but she had a tendency to exaggerate.

"So am I," she said, swiping at her strawberry-blonde curls and pushing them out of her green eyes. "With my wedding coming up, I can't afford any setbacks with my complexion. You should see my beauty routine." She rolled her eyes. "It takes *hours*. What we women subject ourselves to in the name of youth and beauty! It's nuts. At least I can relax when I drink a cup of your tea."

"It's tough," I agreed, with real sympathy. Even though Cherry was in her late twenties and still as cute and perky as she likely was when she was the captain of the Redemption High School cheerleading squad, she was already terrified at the prospect of getting old. She reminded me of the women I used to associate with when I was back in New York—all the rich wives who didn't work and spent their days worrying about being replaced by a younger model when they grew "too old." I wished there was something other than tea I could give her that would make her feel better about aging gracefully.

Alas, even though I was a firm believer that the right tea could pretty much cure anything, that was a little out of my league.

I ran a tea business out of my home, and I grew many of the herbs and flowers I used in my blends in my backyard. While I had a few popular recipes, like my lemon-lavender and Deep Sleep teas, some of my customers wanted specialized blends. Cherry was one of them. Hers was customized to help her skin maintain its youthful appearance.

"Oh," I continued. "I almost forgot. It sounds like congratulations are in order. You've finally set a date!"

Cherry's face faltered. "Well, it's not official. Yet. But that should all change tonight."

"Oh, that's exciting! What's happening tonight?"

She leaned closer to me as if we were in a crowded restaurant rather than my empty kitchen, and she didn't want anyone to overhear us. Well, empty other than Midnight, my black cat, who didn't appear to be listening to us anyway as he napped in the sun. "It's a surprise. All I know is I'm supposed to get dressed up and be ready at 7 p.m. sharp."

"Oooh, a romantic surprise. How fun," I said, feeling a little pang. I immediately pushed it away, though. It was better for everyone if I didn't date. Especially one specific member of the Redemption Police Department named Brandon Wyle.

"I know, I can't wait," Cherry said, tucking the bag of tea into her purse and rooting around for her wallet. Her cheeks had flushed pink, which made her look even more appealing. "Marcus has never done anything like this before, so what else could it be but to finally set the date? And it's perfect timing with Valentine's Day just a few weeks away."

"You did tell me how much he loves making grand gestures," I said.

Cherry nodded as she finally fished her wallet out. "He does," she sighed. "Like the time he threw that surprise birthday party for me. Or when he whisked me off to that romantic bed-and-breakfast for last year's Valentine's Day celebration."

"He's definitely a keeper," I said. Truth be told, I had no idea if he was or not, as I had never even met the man. All I knew was what Cherry shared with me, which on the surface, sounded amazing.

But dig a little deeper, and things weren't quite so rosy. The fact they had been engaged for a while now, at least a couple of years, with no actual wedding date in sight set off more than a few alarm bells. However, it wasn't enough to deter Cherry from closing the deal with him.

"He is," Cherry agreed as she opened her wallet. "You're definitely invited to the wedding. I can't wait for you to meet him. In fact, I'd love for you to be my Bride Whisperer. Anastasia has raved about you."

"Well, I appreciate that," I said, even though I wasn't sure how keen I was to step into that role again. Dealing with one Bridezilla was enough. Plus, I ended up having to solve a murder while carrying out my Bride Whisperer duties.

"You really are the best," Cherry continued as she handed me a few bills. "And I know I should have called you sooner, but it was only yesterday that I realized I had hardly any tea left. It's been so crazy busy; I can't keep anything straight anymore. Between the wedding and work, and now getting ready for this unexpected business trip, it's been madness. Absolute madness."

"I get it," I said, although a part of me wanted to ask her how she, of all people, was complaining about going on a business trip. She was a travel agent, after all. "Luckily, I had all the ingredients ready, so all I had to do was put it together."

"Well, thank you again," Cherry said as she slung her purse over her shoulder. "I hate to run like this, but I still have a million things to do today."

"Oh, well, hold on a second. I need to get you your change." I moved toward my own purse, hoping I had enough singles.

Cherry waved me off. "Don't worry about it. I appreciate you doing this rush job. Besides, I really do have to go. I've got a hot date to get ready for." She winked at me and hurried away, her heels clacking on the kitchen floor as she made her way toward the front door.

Midnight picked up his head and stared at me with his emerald-green eyes. "Don't give me that look," I said. "You and I both know the last thing I need is a romantic surprise date."

He yawned, showing off an impressive array of teeth.

"I'm not going to argue with you," I said, briskly moving into the kitchen. I had a sudden urge to bake a fresh batch of my famous chocolate chip cookies.

Red Hot Murder - Chapter 2

The phone rang, jerking me out of a sound sleep. I fumbled for it, my heart instantly in my throat. At that hour of the night, I automatically assumed it was my sister, Annabelle, calling from New York with terrible news.

But then I reminded myself it was more likely someone like Dana, calling with a middle-of-the-night tea emergency. Again.

"Charlie?" The voice was so choked with tears, I could barely make it out.

"It's me," I said, swinging my legs out of bed as fear started to take hold again. "Who is this?" I almost asked if it was Annabelle, but I wasn't sure if I could get the words past the lump in my throat. Plus, it sounded nothing like my sister. Was it my best friend, Pat? No, it didn't sound like her, either.

"It ... it ... it's me," the voice said between sobs. "Cherry."

"Cherry?" I wasn't sure I'd heard her right.

Cherry burst into a fresh bawl. "You have to come," she said. "He's not moving. You have to help him."

"He? Do you mean Marcus?" My mind raced as I thought about her romantic surprise date. "Is something wrong with Marcus?"

Another hiccup. "Please come. He needs help. I need help."

"Cherry, if there's something wrong with Marcus, call 9-1-1."

"You don't understand," she cried. "I don't remember. He wasn't here. So, I don't even know how he was attacked."

Attacked? What was she talking about? Was she in the middle of a bad trip? Was THAT the romantic surprise? I tugged a hand through my wild, brownish- blondish hair, trying to decide if maybe *I* should hang up and call 9-1-1. "Cherry, what is going on? Talk to me."

"I ca ... can't. Please just come. Hurry." There was a click, and the phone went dead.

I stared at the receiver. Really, the smart move would be to call 9-1-1 myself. I had no business heading over to her house in the middle of the night, especially if I was going to end up in the middle of some dangerous situation. Best to let the professionals take care of it.

Yet ... her voice tugged at me. She sounded terrified ... like something had gone very wrong.

What she really needed was someone in her corner she could trust.

Before I was even aware I had made the decision, I was striding over to my closet to pull on a pair of jeans and an oversized University of Wisconsin sweatshirt. I headed into my en suite bathroom to quickly brush my teeth, wash my face, and try to do something with my wild hair. I finally managed to gather it into a loose ponytail, although a few tendrils had snuck out and were framing my face. I stared at myself in the mirror. My hazel eyes were puffy from lack of sleep, and I looked far older than my early thirties.

Well, it's not like you're going to a party, I scolded myself. *If you're gonna do this, then hurry up and do it.*

I left the bedroom and hurried to find my keys.

* * *

Upon my knock, Cherry immediately opened the door and nearly fell into my arms. "Oh, thank goodness it's you."

She looked dreadful. Her eyes were red and swollen, and her hair, which looked like it had been carefully styled in a complicated up-do, had fallen halfway out. There were black streaks down her face where her makeup had smeared, and black flecks stained her red dress, which was now wrinkled. There was also a huge run in her pantyhose.

"Let's get inside," I said, gently pushing her into her front hallway as I quickly glanced around to see if anyone had seen us. Cherry was renting an apartment on top of a garage. Her landlords were a very sweet, retired couple. The wife was actually one of my tea customers, and the one who had referred Cherry to me. The property was in a quiet neighborhood filled with other retirees. While it was still dark and very much the middle of the night, if there was one thing I knew about older, retired people, it was that they were often up and wandering around at all hours of the night. In many cases, they also liked to take a peek out of their windows to make sure all was quiet in the neighborhood. Until I knew precisely what was going on, I would prefer not to be identified showing up at that particular time.

Cherry's body was limp and pliable as I maneuvered her back into her apartment. I couldn't figure out if it was shock or something else, but I didn't like how she looked. There was a glassiness to her eyes, and her skin was extremely pale.

"Charlie, you have to help him. You have to. I don't know what happened. Nothing makes any sense." The words were tumbling out of her so fast, they were practically on top of one another. Her breathing had sped up so much, she was practically gasping, and I was a little afraid she might hyperventilate.

I took hold of her shoulders and gave her a little shake. "Cherry, calm down. Breathe. I'm here. We'll figure it out, but first you have to breathe for me. Okay? Can you do that?" As much as I wanted to get a look at whoever it was who wasn't moving, I also knew I had to at least calm Cherry down enough to stabilize her before I ended up with two medical emergencies on my hands.

She gulped, her breath catching in her throat, but I could see her trying to mimic my breathing. I kept encouraging her until she finally seemed calm enough to disclose some information.

"Can you tell me what's going on?"

Almost immediately, her agitation accelerated again. "I told you ... I don't remember. Someone must have broken in and attacked him, but I don't remember."

"Okay," I said quickly. "Why don't we go into the kitchen, and I'll make some tea? And you can ..." I was going to say, "tell me where he is," but her eyes went wide, and she started gasping again.

"I can't go in the kitchen," she said, her voice high and panicked. "That's where he is!"

Well, that answered it. "Okay, why don't we go sit down in the living room? And then I can go check on him."

That appeared to be the right solution, as she immediately calmed down again and allowed me to lead her there.

The room was oddly lit, as both lamps were on the floor, but there was enough light to show that it was a disaster. One of the end tables had been knocked over, along with the coffee table. There was a pool of mail and magazines on the floor in front of the latter along with a mug lying on its side, lipstick smeared across its rim. Next to that were two wine glasses, one broken and one with lipstick marks, along with a bright-red phone. The television was also smashed. A gold-framed photo was lying in front of it, and I wondered if that was what had been used to break the screen. It was difficult seeing who exactly was in the photo, as the glass was cracked, but as far as I could tell, it appeared to be a picture of Cherry and a man with curly, black hair.

"I don't know what happened," Cherry said again. Her hands were pressed together at her palms, and she was shaking her head. "I don't understand what's going on."

"Okay, let's just sit down," I said, leading her to the loveseat, which was still intact. I suspected the reason why she had only one chair and a loveseat was because the room was too small for a full-sized couch. I quickly shed my jacket and slung it over the side, trying to keep it out of the way of the wreck. "I promise you, we'll sort this all out, but first I need to go into the kitchen and check on whoever's in there." Cherry's eyes filled with tears, and I hesitated, wondering if she was on the verge of another breakdown. But I also had to know the truth. "So it *is* Marcus?" I asked, my voice as gentle as I could make it.

Her breath caught in her throat, and she nodded.

"Did you call 9-1-1?"

Her eyes widened with horror. "No! No cops. Charlie, you can't call them. I can't talk to them. I don't remember anything."

"Okay, no cops," I cut in, trying to head off another hysterical outburst. "I'll go into the kitchen and see what's going on. I'm going to make you some tea, as well."

She nodded again. I led her to the loveseat and sat her down. I was about to pick up both the lamps and the end table, as then the living room would stop looking like some freaky horror show, but stopped myself at the last second. Surely, the cops wouldn't want anything moved.

Which means the only task left was to check out the kitchen. I took a deep breath and headed in.

I steeled myself before I walked in, more than a little apprehensive about what I would find. If the living room was in shambles, how much worse would the kitchen be, considering the array of weapons and knives within easy reach?

Luckily, my fears turned out to be unjustified. Other than a sink full of dirty dishes and both chairs overturned on the floor, it appeared more or less normal.

Well, other than the body on the floor.

I knelt down next to Marcus, intending to check for a pulse, but I wasn't holding out much hope. One look at him, and it was clear he was dead. When I touched his neck, it was already cold.

Oh no. I felt sick. What had Cherry done?

And what on Earth was I going to do?

For a moment, I could only sit there, staring intently at a man who was just a few years younger than me. Even in death, he was beautiful, with a head of black, silky curls, high cheekbones, and a perfect mouth. Although I couldn't tell for certain, I suspected he was the man in the shattered photo.

Thanks to hours at the gym, his chest was broad and muscular, and he wore dark jeans and a button-down blue flannel shirt. He looked relatively peaceful, and I wondered just what had killed him. Had Cherry poisoned him? I thought of the two wine glasses in the living room. But if he drank poisoned wine there, wouldn't his body be there, too? Why would he have come into the kitchen? Especially since it looked like he and Cherry had one heck of a fight in the other room.

It didn't make any sense.

Well, sitting frozen next to his body wasn't going to get my questions answered. I pulled myself to my feet, trying to decide how to best approach Cherry, when I noticed a pillow next to Marcus's head. Why would there be a pillow there? Was Cherry going to put it under his head? And if that was her intention, why didn't she?

So many questions, and the only person who could answer them was still teetering on the verge of hysteria. I glanced toward the stove, really wanting to make tea, but I also didn't know if I wanted to take the time for that. The sooner I could get through to Cherry, the sooner I could get the cops involved.

Taking another deep breath, I headed back into the living room.

Cherry was still in the same place I'd left her. She was slumped over, her arms dangling between her knees.

Gingerly, I sat down next to her and reached out to take one of her hands. It was frigid, and for a fleetingly second, I was reminded of how cold Marcus was. She inhaled a deep, shuddering sigh when I touched her, and slowly turned her face toward me. "He's dead, isn't he?"

There was no use sugarcoating it. "I'm so sorry."

Her face scrunched up, and I could see fresh tears well up in her eyes. "We were going to get married," she whispered.

I gently squeezed her hand. "I know. I'm so, so sorry for your loss."

She turned her head to stare at the carpet as fat tears began to drip down her face. "We were to get married and have kids and grow old and die together."

I squeezed her limp hand again. There were no words. Unfortunately, that didn't mean there weren't things that needed to be done. And the sooner, the better.

"Cherry," I said very gently. "We need to call the cops."

She shook her head, but a bit less adamantly than before. "No cops." She was like a shell of her earlier self, almost as if my confirming what she knew had drained the hysteria from her body.

"We have no choice," I said. I kept my voice gentle, but I also made it firm. If she thought I was going to help her hide a body, she was going to be sorely disappointed.

She lifted her head to meet my eyes, her face a mask of grief and despair. "You don't understand," she said. "It's like I told you … I don't remember."

"What don't you remember?"

She threw her hands up in the air. "Anything! That's the problem, I don't remember anything." Her voice became agitated again.

"Okay," I said soothingly. Maybe I should have taken the time to make some tea after all. "Why don't you tell me what you DO remember, and we'll take it from there?"

She looked back down at her lap as she took a deep, shuddering breath. "I remember getting ready," she said, her voice soft. "I was so excited. I was sure tonight was going to be the night when we'd finally set a date, and I'd be that much closer to being Mrs. Marcus Whitlock. I had my hair done and spent extra time on my makeup. I was still getting ready when I heard a knock at the door. As you can imagine, I panicked. It was only 6 p.m., and the note had said I should be ready at 7. Had I gotten something wrong? I headed over to the front door, all set to tell Marcus I still needed more time, but there wasn't anyone there."

A shiver of unease reverberated through my body. "No one?"

Cherry shook her head. "No. But there was a package with a single rose on top of it." Her smile was soft at the memory. "It was a box of my favorite dessert … chocolate-dipped strawberries. There was a note, too. 'This is just the beginning of the treats I have in store for you tonight.'"

"Wow," I said. "He really does go all out, doesn't he?"

221

She nodded, another tear leaking out of her eye. "He was amazing. He had this way of treating me like an absolute princess. I felt like I was the only one in the world in his eyes." She swallowed hard.

I squeezed her hand again. "So, then what? You finished getting ready?"

"Yes. Well, after I put the rose in water and had a strawberry. Well, maybe two." She ducked her head, a faint bloom of pink appearing on her face. "I didn't want to spoil my appetite because I was sure whatever Marcus had planned, it would be spectacular. But they were sooo good. I had to force myself to stop. I put the box in the fridge, so I wouldn't be further tempted, and I went back to the bedroom to finish getting ready. The next thing I knew, I found myself on the floor of the living room, and Marcus … Marcus …" Her face scrunched up as more tears streamed down her cheeks.

"It's okay," I said as she started to sob, burying her face in her hands. I wrapped my arms around her shoulders, holding and rocking her as she cried. It took a little bit for the worst to move through her, but when it finally did, I realized she was in need of tissues.

"Wait here," I said, giving her another squeeze. "I'll go find some tissues and make that tea."

She kept her face in her hands as her head bobbed up and down. I stood up and headed back to the kitchen, figuring I would start by getting the water on the stove and then hunt down tissues. I knew I needed to convince Cherry we needed to call the cops, and soon, and I was hoping once she was calmer, she would finally see reason.

I clicked on the kitchen light and nearly gave myself a heart attack seeing Marcus still lying on the floor. It wasn't like I didn't know he was there, but somehow, I didn't expect to see him. Or the pillow lying next to his head. I was going to have to ask Cherry about it.

I moved to the stove where the teakettle sat on one of the back burners. I filled it up, avoiding the pile of dirty dishes in the sink, then figured out how to turn the burner on before hunting around for a couple of clean mugs.

Something was niggling at the back of my head, but I couldn't figure out what exactly was bothering me. I set out the mugs, found the tea, and stood for a moment just looking around the kitchen. Something was off, but ... what?

Of course, it could have just been the dead body and pillow throwing me. I picked my way out of the kitchen and found my way to the bathroom, which was just as messy as the kitchen. The counter was strewn with various makeup brushes, sponges, and potions, along with pink and green streaks of color. A crumpled tissue stained with lipstick was in the sink.

I had no idea Cherry was such a slob.

I picked up the box of tissues sitting on the back of the toilet and went back into the living room to hand it to Cherry. I still couldn't shake the sense that something wasn't right with Cherry's account of the night.

It was only while digging around in the fridge looking for cream or milk to add to Cherry's sugar-loaded tea (to help her get past the shock of what she had been through) that it finally hit me: there WAS something missing.

The box of chocolate-dipped strawberries.

Nor was there a rose anywhere to be found.

I shut the fridge and went back into the living room thinking maybe I'd missed it on the floor, or it was mixed in with the half-broken wine glasses and coffee mug. But as far as I could tell, there was nothing more than the wine glasses and a coffee mug. No rose or vase.

I paused, my brain running through the story Cherry had told me. How was it that the two gifts she mentioned—the rose and the chocolate-dipped strawberries—were nowhere to be found, but two other items—the coffee mug and wine glasses—were never mentioned in Cherry's recounting of the night's events?

Cherry was mopping her face with tissues when I entered the room, but when she saw me standing there, she raised an eyebrow. "Do you need something? Are you having trouble finding things?"

"I was just wondering about the rose. Didn't you say you put it in a vase?"

She gave me a curious look. "Yeah. I left it right …" she pointed to where the coffee table used to be. Her mouth formed a perfect O. "Oh, no. That vase was a graduation present from my grandma. It was Waterford crystal. Don't tell me it's broken."

"No, it's not broken. I just don't see it there."

She stared at me. "What do you mean, there's nothing there? Of course it was there. I remember putting it there last night."

"Well, it's not there now."

"What? That can't be." Cherry craned her neck as she searched the floor.

"But there *are* two wine glasses there," I said. "Do you remember having a glass of wine? Maybe before Marcus got here?"

"Why would I have opened up a bottle of wine if Marcus wasn't here?" she asked as her eyes continued sweeping the floor.

Good question. And now that she had asked it, I realized I hadn't seen an opened bottle of wine in the fridge, either. "What about the coffee mug?"

"Oh!" Her face brightened. "That, I remember. I had some of your tea yesterday. I try and have at least one cup every day. I had just finished it when I heard the doorbell."

Well, that at least cleared up one mystery from the night before. "So you must have brought the empty mug into the living room." Normally, I would have found that strange … especially since Cherry would have walked right by the kitchen on her way to the front door, but after seeing the general lack of housekeeping in the apartment, it was probably not a big surprise a dirty mug might first take a detour into the living room before finding its way into a sink of hot soapy water.

She hesitated, a puzzled look on her face, before looking at me. "No. I'm sure I didn't do that. I would have left it in the bathroom where I was getting ready. I was sipping it while putting on my makeup."

"Is that the mug?" I pointed to where it lay on its side next to the wine glasses.

She frowned. "Ye-e-es." She drew out the word. "But why is it there? And ... where did those wine glasses come from? And where IS my vase? What is going on?" She struggled to get to her feet as the shriek from the tea kettle startled her and caused her to fall back onto the loveseat. I hurried into the kitchen to take care of the tea, leaving Cherry muttering to herself. When I returned, tea mugs in hand, she was on her hands and knees searching through the debris by the coffee table.

"You may not want to touch any of that," I said.

She glanced up, but a hunk of her hair had fallen across one eye, so she gave her head a quick shake to move it out of the way. "Why not?"

"Because the cops will need to investigate."

"No!" She shook her head violently, causing more hair to fall out of her updo. "I told you, no cops!"

Inwardly, I sighed. I had hoped once some time had passed, she would see reason and come to the right conclusion on her own, without me pushing her. But it didn't look like that was going to be the case. I squatted down and wordlessly handed her a mug. She gave me a suspicious look, but took it.

"Cherry," I said after she had swallowed a couple of sips. "You must know we're going to have to get the cops involved. You have a body lying in your kitchen." Her face blanched at that, but I kept going. "It's not like you can leave him there. What would you do with him?"

"I can't have the cops here," she burst out. "I just told you, I don't remember what happened! How am I going to answer their questions if I can't remember anything?"

I tilted my head. "Cherry, do you honestly think if you don't call the cops now, you won't have to answer their questions? What do you think is going to happen when someone realizes Marcus is missing? They're going to call the cops, which means the cops are going to talk to all of Marcus's family and friends." I gave her a pointed look. "Including his fiancé. Who was supposed to have a surprise romantic date night with him the last day anyone saw him." As I talked, Cherry's lips pressed together tighter and tighter until they turned white.

"I know I wasn't the only one you told," I said as gently as I could.

She didn't respond. Instead, she sat back on her heels and took another long drink of tea. It seemed to be working its magic, as she was visibly calming down.

"So, can we call them?"

She lowered her mug until it was resting on her lap. I could see the smear of pink lipstick on the rim, though most of it seemed to have somehow ended up on her chin. "They're going to think I killed him," she said softly, staring into her mug.

I lowered myself to the floor, sitting cross-legged, so I could rest a hand on her knee without tipping over. "Don't you want to know the truth?"

Her face jerked up, her eyes wide. "I didn't kill him. I couldn't! Someone else killed him. Even if he wasn't the love of my life, I don't have it in me to kill *anyone*!" But, despite how sure her words were, I could hear the doubt trembling beneath.

"I know you don't. But something happened here, and we need to get to the bottom of it. We owe it to Marcus. Don't you agree?"

Her shoulders slumped, like she was deflating in front of my eyes, the last vestiges of resistance draining out of her. "You're right. We better call them."

Want to keep reading? Grab your copy of **Red Hot Murder** here:

www.amazon.com/gp/product/B07DT8ZTN3

More *Charlie Kingsley Mysteries:*
A Grave Error (a free prequel novella)
The Murder Before Christmas (Book 1)
Ice Cold Murder (Book 2)
Murder Next Door (Book 3)
Murder Among Friends (Book 4)
Red Hot Murder (Book 6)
A Cornucopia of Murder (Book 7)
A Wedding to Murder For (novella)
Loch Ness Murder (novella)

Secrets of Redemption *series:*
It Began With a Lie (Book 1)
This Happened to Jessica (Book 2)
The Evil That Was Done (Book 3)
The Summoning (Book 4)
The Reckoning (Book 5)
The Girl Who Wasn't There (Book 6)
The Room at the Top of the Stairs (Book 7)
The Search (Book 8)
The Secret Diary of Helen Blackstone (free novella)

Standalone books:
Today I'll See Her (free novella or purchase with bonus content)
The Taking
The Third Nanny
Mirror Image
The Stolen Twin

Access your free exclusive bonus scenes from *The Murder of Sleepy Hollow* right here:

MPWNovels.com/r/q/sleepyhollow-bonus

Acknowledgements

It's a team effort to birth a book, and I'd like to take a moment to thank everyone who helped.

My writer friends, Hilary Dartt and Stacy Gold, for reading early versions and providing me with invaluable feedback. My wonderful editor, Megan Yakovich, who is always so patient with me. My designer, Erin Ferree Stratton, who has helped bring my books to life with her cover designs.

And, of course, a story wouldn't be a story without research, and I'm so grateful to my friends who have so generously provided me with their expertise over the years: Dr. Mark Moss, Andrea J. Lee, and Steve Eck. Any mistakes are mine and mine alone.

Last but certainly not least, to my husband Paul, for his love and support during this sometimes-painful birthing process.

About Michele

A USA Today Bestselling, award-winning author, Michele taught herself to read at 3 years old because she wanted to write stories so badly. It took some time (and some detours) but she does spend much of her time writing stories now. Mystery stories, to be exact. They're clean and twisty, and range from psychological thrillers to cozies, with a dash of romance and supernatural thrown into the mix. If that wasn't enough, she posts lots of fun things on her blog, including short stories, puzzles, recipes and more, at MPWNovels.com.

Michele grew up in Wisconsin, (hence why all her books take place there), and still visits regularly, but she herself escaped the cold and now lives in the mountains of Prescott, Arizona with her husband and southern squirrel hunter Cassie.

When she's not writing, she's usually reading, hanging out with her dog, or watching the Food Network and imagining she's an awesome cook. (Spoiler alert, she's not. Luckily for the whole family, Mr. PW is in charge of the cooking.)

Made in United States
Orlando, FL
17 June 2023

34251243R00134